"He's *my* grandfather, I have a right to see him!"

Tessa's eyes flashed. "What do you think I'm going to do to him, for heaven's sake?"

"You're Todd Mellor's granddaughter, all right," he grated. "Your mother's probably as stubborn or she wouldn't have acted the way she did."

"My mother acted out of love."

"Love?" Unexpectedly Crane kissed her. Tessa's senses reeled at the sensuality of it. "There," he said. "Wouldn't it be all too easy to mistake that for love? You were ready to say yes to anything."

Tessa was shocked into silence.

"The kind of love you talk about is just a con. People get hurt by it, and if I can help it, Todd Mellor's not going to be hurt any more." Crane's eyes snapped. "You see him when I decide."

Tessa's body burned with shame—he was right, she would have said yes.

Nicola West, born on the south coast of England, now lives in central England with her husband and family. She always knew she wanted to write. She started writing articles on many subjects, a regular column in a county magazine, children's stories and women's magazine stories before tackling her first book. Though she had three novels published before she became a Harlequin author, she feels her first novel for Harlequin was a turning point in her career. Her settings are usually places that she has seen for herself.

Don't miss any of our special offers. Write to us at the following address for information on our newest releases.

Harlequin Reader Service
901 Fuhrmann Blvd., P.O. Box 1397, Buffalo, NY 14240
Canadian address: P.O. Box 603,
Fort Erie, Ont. L2A 5X3

Hidden Depths
Nicola West

Harlequin Books

TORONTO • NEW YORK • LONDON
AMSTERDAM • PARIS • SYDNEY • HAMBURG
STOCKHOLM • ATHENS • TOKYO • MILAN

Original hardcover edition published in 1987
by Mills & Boon Limited

ISBN 0-373-02884-9

Harlequin Romance first edition January 1988

Printed in U.S.A.

CHAPTER ONE

HE DOESN'T want me here.

Tessa Walker stared at the words she had just scrawled on the page, half frightened by the sudden savage emotion which had driven her pen across the paper. She hadn't meant to write that at all.

Her heart thumping, she snatched it up and tore it across, throwing the pieces into the waste-paper basket. She'd set out to write a cheerful, reassuring letter to her mother, back home in England. She'd meant to dispel any suspicion that she might not be welcome here, in Arizona. But the words she'd just written—and the ferocity which had jabbed the point of her pen right through the paper as she wrote them—weren't going to do that. They were just going to make matters worse.

It's no use, Tessa thought, leaning her head on her hand and staring out with dejection at the brilliance of the blue sky, the hot red of the desert rocks, the tangle of trees that bordered the rim of the Grand Canyon. That old quarrel isn't going to be mended, just by my coming out here. Why, I haven't even managed to see Grandfather yet—and if Crane has his way, I never will.

'Go to Arizona?' she had echoed, when her mother had first broached the plan. 'Go to the Grand Canyon and visit Grandfather, and get him to make it up? It'll be a waste of time!'

'I don't think so.' Betsy Walker's smile had been tired, but there had been a measure of confidence in it—confidence that Tessa considered completely unfounded. Hadn't her grandfather refused to have any contact with his daughter ever since her runaway marriage, twenty-five years ago? Hadn't he left every letter unanswered? They didn't even know if he'd bothered to open and read them—if he even knew about his grandchildren, Tessa and her brother Stuart, now just about to finish school and go to university. Why should he feel any different just because his granddaughter took it into her head to visit him now?

Tessa gazed at her mother and thought of going all that way, alone—because Stuart couldn't go with her, his 'A' levels just coming up. She thought of finding out where her grandfather lived now, going to his house, knocking on the door—and having it slammed in her face.

That was if he was still alive—but she couldn't say that to her mother.

Ever since Tessa had been old enough to understand, she had known that it was Betsy Walker's dearest wish that the quarrel with her father should be made up. The fact that he'd never been able to accept her marriage to an Englishman—a marriage that took her to the other side of the world—had been the one sorrow in her life, until her husband died at the tragically early age of thirty-six. Betsy had been thirty-five then, and Tessa and Stuart twelve and seven. She might have taken them back to America and thrown herself on her father's mercy; but she couldn't risk a rejection, and she'd elected to stay in England with the many friends she and Mike Walker had made there, and with the support of Mike's own family. None the less, life hadn't been easy, and bringing up the two children while working full-time to support them had taken its toll.

Now, at only forty-five, she was frail, ill with a heart complaint that the doctors had told her would probably result in a shortened lifespan. It was for this reason that she wanted Tessa to go to America and make her peace with Todd Mellor.

'You're the only one who can go,' she said now, reaching out to take Tessa's hand. 'And I'd so much like to know that he hasn't completely forgotten me—that he could still find some love in his heart, after all these years. I'd like him to know that I've never forgotten him. And that your father made me very happy.'

Tessa felt her eyes fill with tears. Her father had died ten years ago, yet she could still feel pain when she thought of him. Her mother was right—they *had* been happy, all of them. And it had been the memory of his love and strength that had helped her mother through the difficult years alone.

'How can I think of leaving you now?' she said to her mother, noting the fragility of the hand she held, the transparency of the skin. 'You need me here to look after you. And——' She stopped, but she knew that Betsy was finishing the sentence in her own mind. *Suppose something happens to you while I'm away.* Words she couldn't speak aloud.

'It's all right,' her mother said calmly. 'I'll still be here when you come back. I've enough time for that. But I'd like you to go soon.'

The tears threatened to spill from Tessa's eyes, and she bowed her head. She knew she would have to go. In this, she couldn't let her mother down.

Arrangements for the trip were made surprisingly quickly,

and it was only a short time before Tessa found herself aboard the plane for Los Angeles. From there, she was to fly on to Las Vegas; she had written to her grandfather to tell him this, without much hope of acknowledgement, and planned to hire a car at the airport and drive the rest of the way to the Grand Canyon.

Her feelings, as the plane flew the last leg of her journey, were mixed. Rather to her surprise, she'd been unable to help a slowly rising excitement at the thought of the trip— her first to America. Now, as she stared down at the desert with its arid dryness broken only by tumbled red rocks, she found her excitement tempered by nervousness at the thought of what lay ahead. And she wondered yet again just what reception she would get from the old man who had allowed bitterness to cloud both his own life and that of his daughter.

'Suppose he's not there any more?' she'd said to her mother. 'Suppose he's moved—left the area?'

'He won't have done that,' Betsy answered confidently. 'Nothing would have made my dad leave the Canyon. He was born there, and always looked on it as his ancestral home—don't forget, his mother was an Indian and her tribe had lived in the Canyon for generations. That's why he hated me leaving it—he believed that we were a part of the land and should stay there. As Joe did, of course.'

'I wonder if he's still there now,' said Tessa thoughtfully. She had heard her mother talk about her family so often that she felt she almost knew her uncle Joe, Betsy's older brother—bluff, hearty, good-humoured. She had never been able to understand why he hadn't contacted his sister, even if their father had been against it. But perhaps he had resented Betsy's marriage as well.

'And Crane,' her mother reminded her. 'You'll probably meet him too—your cousin.' She smiled reminiscently. 'I wonder how he turned out. He was a real individual, young Crane—just twelve when I left but already half-way to being a man. One of those tall, active, well grown youngsters, always out fishing or swimming or hiking. And although he was adopted, there always seemed to be a lot of Joe in him, somehow. I suppose it was because he had Indian blood in him, too—the strong, almost arrogant features, they were showing already. He'll be—oh, let's see, nearly thirty-seven now—my, that seems impossible.'

'He probably left the Canyon and became a big business man somewhere in the city,' Tessa said drily. She had an idea she wouldn't like her adopted cousin Crane much, and hoped they wouldn't have to meet. He sounded just the kind of tough, ruthless man she most disliked.

'I don't think he did, somehow,' Betsy said, thoughtfully. 'He loved the Canyon too much—he seemed to have a kind of affinity with it, as if it were a part of him—or he a part of it. Oh, well——' she gave Tessa a smile '—I guess you're probably right. He grew up to do something quite different. We know one thing, anyway—he never went into films. We'd have heard about him if he did—Crane was going to be the sort of man who'd make quite a mark, whatever he decided to do.'

The plane touched down at Las Vegas, and Tessa gathered her cabin luggage together. She took her make-up purse from her bag and stared into the small mirror, wondering whether her grandfather would like what he saw—if he agreed to see her at all. A small, oval face, pale in spite of the golden tan she always acquired with the first sunny days of summer, with brown eyes that were wide and dark with anxiety. Sighing, she pushed at the gleaming cap of black hair, flicking its feathery edges around her cheeks. Why couldn't she look beautiful and glamorous, like—like that poised, self-assured blonde over the aisle, for instance? Instead of like some French urchin, straight from school?

I have Indian ancestors too, she thought, feeling a sudden unexpected kinship with the grandfather she had never known. His mother was my great-grandmother. She looked again, realising that the dark eyes and hair, the smooth golden skin must have come from that great-grandmother—though not the features, too pixie-like and delicate to have been handed on by that proud race. Will it mean anything to him, that I must resemble her a little?

Though not, apparently, as much as her cousin Crane did, even though there had been no actual blood relationship between them. But he had borne the Indian stamp even as a child, her mother had said. What was he like now, fully grown and mature?

Well, it was unlikely that she would find out. He must almost certainly have left the Canyon and gone to seek his fortune in the city. And he wouldn't want to meet her, any more than she wanted to meet him.

Tessa stood up to join the throng of passengers now filing towards the door of the plane. She was glad of the trips she'd made abroad in the past few years, since leaving school. Her job as a secretary and personal assistant had involved several foreign trips, and although she had never travelled as far afield as this, she was familiar with the universal airport procedures of waiting for luggage, passing through Customs and filling in forms. And as many of the formalities had already been completed at Los Angeles, she found herself going through the barrier into the Arrivals hall sooner than she had expected.

Now to find the car hire offices . . . Tessa glanced around, looking over the heads of the people waiting there for friends and relatives, trying to see a sign which would help her. And to her astonishment, saw instead her own name.

It was written on a large piece of cardboard and held up high by a tall, powerfully built man with hair as black as her own, and strong, craggy features. Tessa stopped and stared, taking in his height, the loose-limbed, relaxed way he had of standing, which did nothing to dispel the suggestion of virile strength coiled inside him like a spring. He reminded her of a wild animal; at rest now, but ready for sudden and devastating action at the slightest hint of a threat.

A threat? But what threat could she be to him? And who could he be?

Tessa moved forward again slowly, reluctant to declare herself, yet knowing she must. She had a deep, uneasy feeling that meeting this man was somehow going to change her life, setting her on a course from which she could never turn back. She was standing at a crossroads; if she took one way, went past him as if the name on his board meant nothing to her, refused to let him into her life—then nothing would change. But once they had touched hands, looked into each other's eyes . . . She shivered.

But almost as quickly as the sensation had touched her, it disappeared. Because she didn't have any choice, did she? She had to tell him she was Tessa Walker, go with him wherever he chose to take her, accept him—even temporarily—as her guide. Because she had promised her mother that she would find Todd Mellor, her grandfather, and this

man would take her to him. He could only know of her
coming through Todd himself—and Todd must have sent
him to meet her.

Tessa straightened and lifted her head. The journey had
disorientated her, she thought, given her strange ideas. Of
course this man could have no effect on her life! She
marched up to him and looked up into his face.

'I think you're waiting for me,' she said clearly, holding
out her hand. 'I'm Tessa Walker.'

The man looked down at her. He was impossibly tall, she
thought with an unreasonable resentment—he must be six
feet three, at least. Not for the first time, she wished she
were not so small—petite, her friends called her, but to
Tessa five feet two was just plain short. And she could
certainly have done with not having to tilt her head so far
back now, just to meet this stranger's eyes.

And what unnerving eyes they were! Dark, so dark a
brown that they were almost black, boring right into her as
if reading every secret recess of her mind—she flinched—
yet giving nothing away. Unreadable in the deeply tanned,
inscrutable face. Tessa felt another shiver goose across her
flesh. She had never, she thought, seen such implacability.
He could have been carved from stone, and looked just
about as pliable. She hoped that once he had taken her to
her grandfather she wouldn't have to see any more of him.

Realising that she was still holding out her hand, as still
as if she too were carved from stone, Tessa began to
withdraw it. But the stranger prevented her. His scrutiny
apparently over, he took her hand in his, and at his touch
Tessa felt a shock run through her body, as if she had been
grasped by a live wire. Her hand felt lost in the massive
strength and she massaged it with relief when he let her go.

'So you're Tessa,' he said, his voice deep and slow, with a musical quality that was totally unexpected. 'Little Cousin Tessa.' Strong white teeth showed briefly in a smile as Tessa's eyes widened in surprise. 'Yes, I'm your cousin,' he drawled with an odd twist to the firm, uncompromising line of his mouth. 'Crane Mellor—at your service.' The bow was as ironical as his tone. 'And you've come all the way from England to visit with us—well, how about that!'

Tessa dragged herself together. She would try to sort out her tumbled thoughts later. The main thing now was not to let him intimidate her.

She planted her feet more firmly and lifted her head a little higher. 'That's right,' she said coolly. 'I'm little Cousin Tessa, all the way from England. It's good of you to come and meet me, Crane.'

He shrugged. 'I had to come to Vegas anyway,' he said, implying that he wouldn't have made a special journey for her. 'It was a good thing your plane wasn't late—I don't have too much time to waste.' He bent and lifted her two suitcases. 'This way.'

He turned and was gone into the crowd before Tessa could catch her breath. So that was his idea of a welcome! she thought, scurrying after the tall, rangy figure. Didn't he have any idea what it was like, arriving in a strange country after a journey that had taken nearly a whole day? Probably not—he'd evidently spent the whole of his life in and around Arizona. Looking at his clothes, casual to the point of being scruffy, it seemed quite certain that he hadn't made his mark in a city job—or, indeed, anywhere.

All muscle and no brain, she thought scornfully, as they left the airport buildings. The heat hit her—she staggered slightly, gasping at the searing blaze of the sun, but Crane didn't seem to notice. He simply strode on, not even looking round to see if she were following, apparently making for an empty space of the airfield.

Tessa spurted after him.

'Where are we going?' she panted when she caught him up. 'I want to go to the Grand Canyon—to visit my grandfather. I can quite easily hire a car. You don't have to take me——'

'I'm taking you to the Canyon, don't worry.' His voice was laconic, as if his words were valuable, too valuable to waste on her. He jerked his head. 'My plane's over there. It's a mite faster than using the road.'

'Your *plane*?' Tessa stared out over the shimmering runways, trying to make out objects through the heat-haze. Yes, there were several small planes there, lined up as if waiting for a race to start. 'One of those is yours?' she asked, beginning to revise her ideas about him. Surely, even in America, you had to be fairly well-off to own a plane?

'More'n one.' He hadn't slackened his pace, and Tessa found herself having to half run to keep up with him. 'I've got six altogether, plus a couple of choppers—two are down here for servicing, one I'm flying back—the others are back at the Canyon.'

'The Canyon?' Tessa shook her head. They were quite close to the planes now and Crane was heading for a pair of bright red ones at the end of the line. There was something written on the side, but he had the door open before Tessa could read it, and was motioning her to climb inside.

'That's right.' He stowed the luggage away, then swung himself easily into the pilot's seat beside her and began to stare at the instrument panel—an array of switches, lights and meters that looked too complicated for Tessa ever to understand, even in this small aircraft. She twisted round to look inside it.

The cabin was completely open, so that the pilot could talk to the passengers, and there was room for six people. Wide windows stretched down the sides of the plane. There was no gangway; the double seats could be reached only from outside doors, and once you were in there was no way of moving about.

'But what do you do with aeroplanes at the Grand Canyon?' she asked. 'Ferry people about—to Las Vegas and other places? Don't most people come in cars, or coaches?'

'Sure they do.' He had finished his check of the instruments and turned to look down at her. Tessa caught the jet gleam of his eyes. Yes, he definitely showed his Indian ancestry, she thought, feeling an odd shiver run down her spine. Stern, craggy profile, hawk-like nose, sleek black hair that shone like a raven's wing—it was all there. And although in his check shirt and faded jeans he looked completely American, it wasn't hard to imagine him in full Indian regalia, complete with feathered head-dress—Chief of a proud and ancient tribe. He would, she knew instinctively, have to be Chief.

His eyes were on her now as if at last he could spare the time to direct his thoughts towards her. Tessa knew at once that they weren't favourable. How could they be? Her mother's father had probably poisoned the whole family against his rebellious daughter—and so against her. Her heart sank. It had been a waste of time coming here, just as she'd known it would be. So why didn't Crane tell her that straight away, instead of going through this farce of taking her to the Canyon? Why hadn't he written to tell her, so that she needn't have come at all?

'I run a flight of planes into the Canyon itself,' he said, answering the question she'd almost forgotten asking. 'There are only four ways of seeing it, you know—by foot, hiking down into it on one of the trails, by mule—the same way, by raft—running down the river like Powell did when he first explored it, way back, or by air. That's what I do. Take people through by air, so they can say they've seen parts it's impossible to reach. Gives 'em quite a thrill.'

'Yes, I should think it would.' Tessa tried to remember all that she'd read about the Grand Canyon, its vastness, the ruggedness of its towering cliffs, the labyrinths of its inner canyons. 'I should think it's a spectacular flight,' she said politely.

Crane gave her a sharp glance. 'I guess you could say that,' he agreed briefly, and then turned away, absorbing himself once more in the instrument panel. A moment later, the engines roared into life, almost deafening Tessa, who hadn't expected them to be so noisy. She glanced at Crane, but he was still absorbed, and she resigned herself to being battered by the noise all the way to the Canyon. Obviously, there was nothing to be done about it. And at least she wouldn't have to try to make conversation. Later, she would have to ask about her grandfather, but for the time being she had a respite.

'There you are,' Crane shouted a while later, when the steady roar of the engines seemed to Tessa to have become a part of her that she would never be rid of. 'That's the Canyon. Straight ahead.'

Tessa stared in front of her and saw a slash of tawny colour across the arid whiteness of the desert, rimmed with dark green trees and clearings spattered with buildings.

That must be Grand Canyon Village, and not far away from there her grandfather lived... Tessa's nervousness returned, but she didn't have time to think about it. For the Grand Canyon was now in full view and, like everyone else who has seen it, from the very first explorers to the most blasé of present-day travellers, she was temporarily speechless.

Crane had turned the plane so that they were flying above the Canyon, tracing its line through the desert. Tessa stared down in awe, gazing at the thirteen-mile-wide rift in the earth's crust. But it wasn't just a cleft, she realised, not just a gigantic, empty ditch. There was a whole, separate world down there between those rearing cliffs—a world of mountain ranges, of towering hills the size of Ben Nevis, shaped fantastically like Indian temples, with domes and turrets and minarets . . . It was like a landscape laid out by some megalomaniac who desired to rule his own created world, laid out and then abandoned. Because, even in spite of the roar of the aeroplane's engines, Tessa could not fail to be aware of the Canyon's own brooding and impenetrable silence. You could lose London down there in those deep shadowy valleys, she thought, and several other major cities besides.

Crane was taking the plane deeper into the Canyon, flying above the green ribbon that Tessa knew must be the Colorado River, snaking its way along the floor a mile below the rim. Fascinated, she stared down at bare rocks, massive trees, foaming rapids. She looked at the soaring cliffs and towering mountains, rearing high above them now; they were striped and banded with colour from white to deep, rosy red and purple.

And then her awe turned to terror as the tiny plane

corkscrewed its way between the jutting cliffs. Overhanging rocks loomed at them, threatening masses of unyielding boulder that there seemed no way of avoiding until Crane swung the plane aside with a sickening lurch. Unconsciously, she clung to her seat, staring rigidly at the scene that rose and fell before her, plateaux capsizing, vertical cliffs tilting dangerously as if in an earthquake. At one moment she was staring ahead at a massive red mountain, then it had swung away and she found herself gazing down a deep, narrow fissure with water tumbling in a long, straight fall down the gully to the floor of the canyon far below. And then, before she could catch her breath, they were heading for the mouth of a deep, black cavern, and only when she was convinced they were going to fly straight into it did the plane swerve aside and she heard Crane's low chuckle beside her at her gasp.

He was enjoying it, she realised, showing off his skill at flying, handling the plane with casual ease, like a fast car, and finally, with an oblique glance at her, turning it to zigzag back to the wider reaches of the main Canyon.

Tessa found that she was gripping her seat so tightly that her fingers needed almost to be prised loose.

Shaking, she turned to Crane. 'You did that on purpose! Are you mad? We could have been killed.'

'Could we?' To her fury, he sounded amused. 'You know about flying, do you?'

'Enough to know that we could have crashed at any moment in there. Those rocks——'

'You know about the Canyon, too, do you? Flying it? You've been here before? Spent your life here? Flown it every day for the past ten years?'

'Of course I haven't!' Tessa's terror had now turned

entirely to rage. 'But I——'

'Well, I have.' Crane was taking the plane back through the Canyon now, flying smoothly just below the rim, and in spite of her anger Tessa was once more overawed by the grandeur all about her. 'So I suggest you leave the flying to me, OK? A lot of people pay a hundred dollars or more, and gladly, for the experience you've just had. But maybe it means nothing to you. It's just a ditch, after all—a hole in the ground. Couldn't possibly compare with little old England.'

Tessa heard the sarcasm in his voice and bit her lip. She wanted to make an angry retort, tell him that no, none of this could compare with anything in England. But she couldn't do it. She couldn't deny the awesome magnificence of the tawny mountains, sunk in this gigantic gash in the surface of the world. And she couldn't in any way compare it with the soft folds of the Sussex Downs, back home.

'You could at least have warned me,' she said, dismayed to find that her voice sounded merely sulky now. 'I'm sure I would have appreciated it very much—at the right time. Straight after an eighteen-hour journey from London isn't the right time, that's all.'

'My apologies, I'm sure.' Crane bowed ironically in his seat. 'I guess I'll cut out the rest of the tour, then, and take you right home. If that suits you, of course.'

Within minutes, they had left the Canyon behind and were approaching a small airfield close to a sprawling village. Tessa could see other planes and a few helicopters. All for taking trips over the Canyon, she supposed, and wondered if she would have another opportunity to take one. What Crane had shown her—spectacular though it had been—was, she suspected, nothing more than a taste.

'Well, here we are.' The plane had touched down and come to a stop, and Crane switched off the engines. 'Tusayan. This is where I live.'

'Where you live?' Tessa stepped thankfully from the plane and looked around her. 'In the village we just flew over?'

'On the edge of it.' Crane lifted a hand to greet a man who was emerging from some hangars and walking towards them. He wore mechanic's overalls and there was grease on his forehead. But he had a pleasant, open face, Tessa thought, and a friendly smile.

'Just check her over, Em,' Crane said casually. 'She should be OK—the service went smoothly. Everything all right here?'

'No problems.' He was a few years younger than Crane, Tessa guessed, with untidy fair hair. He stood looking at them both, tossing a spanner gently from hand to hand, and Tessa heard Crane give a faint sigh.

'This is my cousin, Tessa Walker,' he said resignedly, and Tessa found a pair of bright blue eyes turned on her as if the young man considered he now had permission to examine her. 'Tessa, this is Emery Mackay, my right-hand man and best friend. Only one thing to beware of—he's insatiably curious. Let him get started and he'll have your life history in five minutes flat.'

'A little longer than that, Crane,' Emery protested with a grin. 'There's usually quite a lot to find out.'

'Not about me, I'm afraid,' Tessa said, liking Emery Mackay and feeling more relaxed than she had since her arrival in America. 'I've had a very dull life.'

'Which she has no time to tell you about now,' Crane said smoothly, and placed his hand on her shoulder. Tessa quivered at the contact and knew that he must feel it; she moved sharply away. 'I'm taking her right back to the house now to have a rest and something to eat. I'll just get your bags out, Tessa, and we'll be away.'

Emery gave Tessa a quirky grin. 'That's your cousin Crane for you,' he said cheerfully. 'No time to stand and stare... OK, I'll check the plane over right away. We don't have any more flights this afternoon.' He nodded at Tessa. 'See you later, Tess. Enjoy your stay.'

Tessa smiled back, thankful that there was someone who apparently didn't hate her on sight. Not that she was being quite fair to Crane in that—he didn't so much hate her, she suspected, as feel totally indifferent to her. And why should he feel anything else? He probably hadn't even known of her existence until a few days ago ...

Following Crane, she climbed into the passenger seat of the long, roomy car that was standing by one of the hangars. Her nervousness had returned. Presumably he would now take her to wherever her grandfather lived— and so far she hadn't had a chance to ask a single question about him.

Crane didn't seem disposed to talk. He started the engine and swung the car out on to the road.

All right, Tessa thought angrily. So you're the strong, silent type. But you're going to have to do some talking now.

She cleared her throat. 'Mind if I ask a few questions?' 'Go right ahead.'

His tone was less than encouraging, but Tessa determined to take no notice. For heaven's sake, she was here, wasn't she? There were things she needed to know.

'My grandfather—how is he?' The question sounded

inane, but she had to start somewhere.

'Pretty well, all things considered.'

'What things? What do you mean?'

'Things you don't know anything about,' he said brusquely, and Tessa felt her cheeks flame.

'And how *would* I know anything about them?' she demanded hotly. 'Since no one's ever thought fit to write and tell us.'

Crane turned his head and glanced down at her, an oblique, dismissive glance that seemed to sum her up and find her wanting. Tessa's skin burned.

'Look, I don't know how much you know about my mother's situation,' she said tersely, 'but she wrote regularly. She never wanted to be cut off from her family. It's just about broken her heart, all these years.'

'So? It was her choice.'

His abrupt words seemed to set the final flaring touch to an anger that had been smouldering in Tessa ever since she had first seen him in the airport. The way he had looked at her in that first moment—every word he had spoken since, every nuance, every tone, all told her that he was against her from the start—her firm and implacable enemy. He had been poisoned by an old man's bitterness—poisoned by something that had happened before she was born. The sheer, illogical injustice of it almost took her breath away, leaving her speechless. But not for long. Tessa was rarely short of words to express what she felt.

'*Her choice?* You think she had a choice of any kind, once she'd met my father—once she'd fallen in love? Of *course* she had to go with him, wherever he went. Even if it meant leaving her family and home. For goodness' sake, it's not *that* unusual, is it? Thousands—millions—of women do it. It's part of life—it's normal.'

'I see. It's all down to love, is it? The great passion that can't be denied.'

His voice was more cuttingly sarcastic than she had yet heard it. She flinched, but wouldn't give way.

'Yes, it is. And it isn't only women—men will do it too. Because, in the end, it's the only thing that matters.'

'Love is?'

Tessa looked at him. He was staring straight ahead, as if driving the car along the quiet road took all his attention. But there had been something in his voice that was even more disturbing than the sarcasm that had bitten at her a few moments before.

'Yes,' she said quietly. 'Love *is* the only thing that matters, in the end. And if you happen to fall in love with someone who lives nine thousand miles away—well, someone's got to move.'

Crane put his foot on the brake and steered the car to the side of the road, running on to the low bank that bordered it. He switched off the engine with a savage flick of his wrist and turned to stare at her.

'You really believe that?' he asked, and his voice was low, throbbing with some powerful emotion that Tessa couldn't identify. 'You really believe that love is that strong—and that it matters that much?'

Tessa tried not to shrink back in her seat. He was so big, there was such a vibrant force emanating from him, she felt he was capable of anything. But he wasn't moving, just staring at her with those dark, almost satanic eyes that seemed to see right down into her soul . . . She took hold of herself. Big he might be, but hadn't she learned to take care of herself? And there was nothing he could do to her here, in broad daylight.

'Yes, I do believe it,' she said staunchly. 'Why not?'

'Why not?' He gave a short, humourless laugh and turned away, staring ahead through the windscreen. 'Because it just isn't true, that's why not. It's a fairytale, don't you realise that? A story, made up to entertain the kiddies on a wet afternoon. The reality's different.' His face was grim, as implacable as the rocks of the Canyon itself. 'Reality's a sort of madness—something that splits families down the middle—leaves everybody hurt.' His voice had dropped as if he were talking to himself, and he seemed to shake himself suddenly and remember where he was. He turned and gave Tessa a searing glance. 'If that's love, I don't want any part of it,' he said harshly. 'It's not my idea of it.'

'And what *is* your idea of it?' Tessa asked quietly, watching him.

'My idea? Why, just two people settling down in the place where they live and making a home and raising a family the way they always did.' He spoke impatiently. 'You don't have to travel half-way across the world to find the right one—the right one can be there on your doorstep. Just so long as you forget all that romantic rubbish and concentrate on the real things—common sense, a good nature and a bit of natural, human warmth.'

And what would *you* know about human warmth? Tessa wondered, but she kept her thoughts to herself. She was beginning to think that Crane had a lot of strange ideas, which he wasn't going to change now, just for her. And anyway, she was too tired to argue. She just wished he would start the engine again and take her to her grandfather, so that she could get the meeting over. It didn't seem that it was going to be a pleasant one.

'And is that how you picked your wife?' she asked coolly.

The response was startling. It seemed that she had asked just the right question to get Crane moving again. With a flick of a glance at her, he twisted abruptly in his seat and started the engine again. His face was dark, the lines set grimly, as he jerked the car back on to the road. They had reached and passed the statutory speed limit before he spoke, and his voice was harshly abrupt.

'I'm not married. Never have been. I've seen enough of it in other people.'

Tessa looked at him and sat back. So that was his trouble. He was a cynic—bitter. He had probably been hurt at some time in his life—and since then had built a thorny barrier around himself.

Well, if that was the way he wanted to live, so be it. Tessa was the last person to try to coax him out of it. And the sooner he dropped her off at her grandfather's house and left her to get on with what she had come to do—mend the rift between Todd Mellor and his daughter Betsy—the better.

The car stopped in front of a long, low, opulent-looking bungalow. Crane got out and began to lift out Tessa's luggage, and she climbed stiffly to her feet, feeling suddenly exhausted in the heat and looking at him doubtfully.

'Is this where Grandfather lives?' Somehow, she hadn't expected such obvious luxury.

Crane shook his head. 'Nope. This is my humble shack. I thought you'd need to unwind a bit before you go on to Grandpa's—jet lag can be pretty fearsome and you need a couple of days to get over it.' He grabbed a case in each hand and jerked his head towards the white walls. 'Come on in.'

Still dubious, Tessa followed him, surprised that he should concern himself about her jet lag—he certainly hadn't seemed in any other way concerned about her!—and by no means sure that she wanted to spend any time at all in his home. She wondered how far away her grandfather lived, and whether this wasn't just a way of delaying their meeting.

'You don't have to have me here,' she announced, feeling instant relief as they came into the shady living-room. 'I mean, I can quite easily put up in a hotel or something. I was quite prepared to do that anyway—I didn't expect Grandfather to feel like asking me to stay.'

Her words sounded ungracious, she knew, but she was suddenly too weary to care much. Unaware of how defenceless she looked, she stood in the middle of the spacious room, looking up at the big, dark man who had brought her here. He looked strong, capable, his very size suddenly reassuring, and for a dizzy moment she wondered just what it would be like to rest against that broad chest, gathered close by those strong arms . . .

Crane gazed down at her and something moved behind his eyes, some flicker of emotion she couldn't define. And then it was gone, and they were as cool and hard as before, like deep brown stones hewn from the depths of the earth.

'You'll stay here,' he said harshly, as if the roughness of his tones could crush feelings he didn't want to acknowledge. 'All right, Grandpa never asked you to come and neither did I. But you're here now and *you're* family——' he shrugged '—for what that's worth. And until—and if—I take you to see Grandpa, you'll be my guest, OK? And no more nonsense about motels.'

'*If* you take me to see Grandfather?' Tessa stared at him, blinking, her eyes almost too heavy now to stay open. 'What do you mean—*if*? And why do you have to take me anyway? Can't I go alone? Do I have to have you along— as nursemaid or something?' The word triggered off another thought and she added with a quick throb of panic, 'He's not ill, is he? Not in—in hospital, or anything like that?'

Crane shook his head with maddening slowness.

'No, Grandpa's not ill,' he drawled, his eyes sardonic. 'But he doesn't live around here. Fact is, he doesn't live up here on the Rim at all. He lives way down in the Canyon, all by himself.'

Tessa stared at him. 'In the *Canyon*?'

'That's right. It's a couple of days' hike to reach him, where he is. And it's not a hike you can make on your own. You're going to have to wait around for someone to take you—for me to take you. And I'm just not sure when that might be.' His dark eyes taunted her. 'Seems like you're stuck here for a while. Sorry—but there it is.'

CHAPTER TWO

RESTLESSLY, Tessa thrust away the sheet of writing paper and stood up. The bedroom, spacious and comfortable though it was, was suddenly claustrophobic—a trap, a prison in which Crane had very effectively incarcerated her. She walked across to the window and stared moodily out.

'You're still suffering from jet lag,' Crane had reminded her inexorably when she'd asked him at lunch time when they could visit Todd. 'It takes time to get over it, you know. And you still look exhausted,' he'd added cruelly.

And that was something he hadn't needed to say, Tessa thought resentfully, looking in the mirror at her still pale face and shadowy eyes. Even a good twelve hours' sleep in that marvellously wide bed hadn't wholly refreshed her. All the same, she thought he was making rather too much of any fatigue she might be feeling. It was certainly beginning to look as if he didn't want her to meet Todd—didn't want her here at all. And, knowing that she couldn't possibly write and tell her mother that, Tessa began to feel very lonely.

'I can't stay here for ever, you know,' she'd told Crane crossly as they ate the salad already prepared and left in the refrigerator by Crane's daily housekeeper. 'And since Grandfather obviously knows I'm coming—or *you* wouldn't have known—I can't see why I shouldn't see him straight away. You're not his keeper, are you?' A thought struck her and she gave him a suspicious look. 'I suppose he *does* know? I suppose you haven't been keeping his letters back—reading them yourself? After all, we didn't even know he'd moved—Mum's been writing to the same address for years.'

'That didn't matter,' Crane said comfortably. 'The letters got passed on OK—everyone knows Todd Mellor. And no, to put your cynical mind at rest, I haven't been hijacking Grandpa's letters. I've read one or two, yes—but only because he showed them to me. And one was the one you wrote, saying you were coming. So yes, he knows—and no, we won't be going there today.'

Tessa stared at him, baffled. 'But why not?' Her anger grew. 'Look, he *is* my grandfather—which is more than you can say. I've a right to see him. And I don't see why I have to wait for your permission, your guidance or anything else. Tell me his address and I'll just go!'

Crane's face had hardened at her reference to the fact that he was adopted. Now, lean and arrogant, it looked as if it had been carved from granite. His eyes were flinty and his voice harsh as he answered.

'You really do think the sun rises and sets around you and your opinions, don't you?' he marvelled. 'You and your ma—you really take the biscuit. She ups and leaves her pa for a man who lives on the other side of the world, and thinks a few letters are all that's needed to keep his heart from breaking—and you breeze along twenty-three years later and expect to find the welcome mat laid out, and yellow ribbons round every tree on the Rim of the Grand Canyon. And all because of a drop of blood.' He stood up and Tessa was alarmed to see that his body was trembling with passion. 'OK, so I don't have just that particular kind of blood in my veins—but I've looked on Todd Mellor as my Grandpa since I was six years old—and he's treated me like his own flesh for over thirty years. I reckon we've been as close as any two human beings can get, blood or no blood. And I'll tell you something else——' He was bending now, his angry face close to hers, cheek twitching, eyes glittering '—I'll do all in my power to see that he doesn't get hurt any more. And if that means preventing you from going to see him—I'll do just that. I don't care if you've travelled from the moon to get here—you get to see your grandfather if and when I say so, and not at all if that's the way I decide!'

Tessa gazed at him. Her own body was beginning to tremble as much as his. Suddenly, she felt that if she didn't put some distance between them, she would be overpowered by the sheer force of his personality, not to mention the shock-waves of almost physical anger that vibrated from his taut body. Pushing back her chair, she scrambled to her feet and backed away.

'If and when you say so! If *you* decide! And just who *are* you, Crane Mellor, to imagine that you can tell me what to do?' Her eyes flashed as furiously as his and she was breathing quickly, still all too well aware of his size and power as he followed her across the room. 'Let me remind you again, he's *my grandfather* and I don't think anyone, not even you, has any right at all to prevent me from seeing him. What do you think I'm going to *do* to him, for heaven's sake?' Pinned against the wall now, she lifted her chin and glowered up into the satanic face. 'Does he know that you're acting as his keeper?' she demanded. 'Does he realise that you've taken it upon yourself to vet his visitors—even members of his own family? I'd bet one of your aeroplanes to a banana-skin that he doesn't! And I should think it's a pretty safe bet that he wouldn't like it at all if he did. Not if what I've heard about him is correct!'

Crane stared down at her. He was so close now that his chest brushed the tips of her breasts, and Tessa was dismayed to feel a tingling that started at the point of contact and spread slowly through her whole body. If only he would move away! But Crane didn't seem to have any intention of doing that. His eyes lanced into hers, midnight-black, and Tessa shivered at their ruthlessness. But she refused to give way, and met their gaze with a directness that seemed to surprise him.

'Well, there's one thing,' he grated at last, 'you sure are Todd Mellor's granddaughter. There's no mistaking that obstinate streak—and I suppose your mother has it too, or she wouldn't have acted the way she did.'

'My mother acted out of love,' Tessa said quietly. The explosiveness seemed to have gone from their quarrel now, although Crane hadn't moved away and she was still acutely aware of his closeness. 'All right, so you don't believe in it—or so you say. But just answer me this——' She met his eyes again, squarely and without fear '—what's your protectiveness of my grandfather if it isn't love? Why do you think so much of him—or he, presumably, of you? Love isn't just sex between a man and a woman, you know. It has a lot more faces than that.'

To her surprise, she caught a flicker of a change in Crane's stony expression then—almost a softening, she thought in wonder. And then it was gone, replaced by a hard scorn that appalled her. Before she could protest, he had raised one hand, cupping the back of her neck and drawing her towards him. With his other hand, he held her waist, the long fingers splayed out, firm against her ribs. And as their bodies came together with a shock that stopped her breath, he bent and laid his mouth on hers.

Tessa's senses reeled. The kiss was so unexpected—and so totally unlike anything she could have expected. If anyone had asked her to guess how Crane Mellor would kiss, she would have had no hesitation in answering—roughly, brutally, demandingly, selfishly. But it wasn't like that at all. His lips were firm but gentle, moving on hers with a sensuousness that had her whimpering softly, all resistance gone. His hands were moving on her body in a caress so tender that she could no more have stopped him than she could have flown his aeroplane through the Grand Canyon. And when he removed his lips from hers and looked into her fluttering eyes, she could only sigh and nestle against him, all her animosity towards him forgotten in the sheer delight of the moment.

'There,' Crane said, and there was an odd huskiness in his voice. 'Now, wouldn't it be all too easy to mistake that for love?'

Tessa stared at him uncomprehendingly.

'You don't know what I mean, do you?' he said slowly. 'You really don't know.' He twisted away and strode to the other end of the room. 'You don't understand that the kind of love you talk about, the kind you say your mother and father had, is just one big confidence trick. Look——' He wheeled round, back at her side before she could move, and Tessa felt herself cowering. If he kissed her again . . . But he didn't. He stared down at her, not touching her. 'Look— when I kissed you just then, you were ready to give way, you'd have said yes to anything—wouldn't you?' He shook his head impatiently at her denials. 'Oh yes, you would, and we both know it. Yet I think you'll agree that there isn't a spark of love between us—not the tiniest flicker, right?' His lips were grim with satisfaction as she nodded mutely. 'So what was it? Just a con, like I said. It's meaningless. Oh, pleasant enough, I agree—but strictly for kicks. As long as you can understand that, you'll be all right in this world. You won't get hurt. And that's what I'm concerned with— not getting hurt. And that goes for Grandpa too. He's been hurt enough—and I make it my business to see that he isn't hurt any more.' His eyes snapped. 'So what I said just now still goes—you see him if and when I say so—and not before.'

Tessa watched as he slammed his way from the room. A few moments later, she heard him start up his car and scream off back to the airfield.

Slowly, feeling as stiff as if she had been pinned to the wall for hours rather than minutes, she moved away and sank shakily into a chair. Almost unconsciously, she rubbed her lips. They felt bruised, in spite of the gentleness of his kiss, almost as if he had bitten them. Her breath was still coming quickly, her heart still racing.

Nobody had ever kissed her in quite that way, with that degree of sensuousness. Crane was clearly an experienced man—taking his pleasure where he found it, she thought sourly, and never confusing it with love. And presumably the women he chose for his—adventures—were as experienced as he, and knew just where they stood.

But that didn't explain her own reaction. It didn't explain why, the moment he touched her, her bones turned to water and her muscles to marshmallow. It didn't explain why she'd responded to his kiss, why she'd wanted it to go on—why, as he'd so rightly sensed, she would have said 'yes to anything'.

Tessa felt her body burn with shame. How *could* she have been so abandoned, so oblivious? What did Crane Mellor—whom she had no reason to like—have that other men didn't? Why should he, of all people, affect her like this?

Well, she thought grimly, getting up, forewarned is forearmed. It won't happen again. And now that I know he really doesn't want me to see Grandfather—that he'll stop me if he possibly can—well, it's up to me.

She looked out of the window. The airfield was out of sight but, as she watched, a small red and white plane lifted from behind the trees and flew off towards the Canyon. That was Crane, taking another group of tourists for a flight along the Rim.

Tessa left the house quickly. If she moved fast, she could get to the airfield and talk to Emery before Crane came back. Emery would know her grandfather's address and how to get there—and she could be on her way before Crane knew anything about it.

Let him stop her seeing her own grandfather! Tessa set her lips firmly. She wasn't Todd Mellor's granddaughter for nothing.

'Well, I dunno.' Emery twisted a lump of cotton waste between his fingers. He looked uncertain, even unhappy. 'I know Crane was meaning to take you himself, I dunno if I ought——'

'Please, Emery,' Tessa begged. They were sitting together inside the hangar and Emery had just handed her a mug of coffee. 'It's obvious how busy Crane is and I really don't want to wait around for too long—Grandfather must be wondering why I don't come. He knew when I was due to arrive. Just tell me where he lives and how to get there, that's all I'm asking.'

'Well, it just ain't so easy as that.' Emery stared out of the hangar door, almost as if hoping for rescue. 'I mean, it's not like he lived on a street and I could give you a number. He's right down in the Canyon and it's a fair old hike—I dunno if you'd ever find it on your own.'

'I'm used to walking. I go up on the South Downs every weekend.' Tessa caught the scepticism in Emery's eyes. 'Honestly, Emery, I'm tougher than I look. Now—I've brought a map of the Canyon floor from Crane's house— just show me where Todd lives and I won't worry you any more.'

Emery sighed as she opened out the map and spread it on the rickety table. 'Well, I suppose it can't do no harm to show you,' he admitted reluctantly. He laid a dirty forefinger on the map. 'Mr Mellor lives just about there, see, at the end of that trail—it don't go nowhere else. But I really don't think you ought to try going down there on your own, Tessa. I mean, I dunno what your—South Downs, is that what you called them? —well, I dunno what they're like but I don't reckon they'll be anything like the Canyon. You ought to wait for Crane, you did really.'

'Well, perhaps I will,' Tessa soothed him. 'But at least I know now where Grandfather lives.' She finished her coffee and stood up. 'Thank you very much, Emery. And don't worry—I shan't do anything silly.'

'I hope you won't.' Emery stared at her, his fair hair ruffled, blue eyes anxious. 'Because if you do and anything happens—well, Crane won't pull his punches, I can tell you. And we've been mates a long time, me and Crane—I wouldn't want anything to spoil it now.'

'Nothing will,' Tessa assured him cheerfully. 'After all, what have you done? Just shown me where Grandfather lives, that's all. And now I'll let you get back to work—I can see you've got a lot to do.' She rolled up the map and gave him a cheerful wave. 'Have a nice day!'

'Have a nice day,' Emery returned glumly, and Tessa departed, laughing.

Now that she was actually doing something, she felt a good deal better. This would show Crane that she wasn't prepared just to sit around awaiting his pleasure! She smiled at the thought of his reaction when he discovered that she had already gone to see her grandfather—for that was what she intended to do, no matter what she'd told Emery. It was better that he shouldn't know—she didn't want to get him into any trouble—but Crane Mellor didn't frighten *her*.

Getting from Tusayan to the Rim took a little time, but Tessa caught a bus and soon found herself wandering around amongst the throngs of visitors. Many of them were dressed for hiking, in shorts and heavy boots, carrying rucksacks, and she eyed these doubtfully. In her hurry, she hadn't brought anything at all, thinking that she could simply call on her grandfather this afternoon and then, if he agreed, move in to stay with him the next day. If he didn't agree—well, she'd face that hurdle when she came to it. She'd always known that it was likely to take time to win him round.

The main thing now was to find the way down. Still confident of her ability to make the journey, Tessa found her way to Mather Point—and then stood quite still.

The Canyon had looked enormous from the air. Here,

standing on the very edge of the plunging cliffs, she could barely take in the immensity of it, the stretching width with its ranges of inner canyons, mountains and precipices. Her eyes were drawn downwards, to the dizzy drop that fell away from below her feet to the winding ribbon of the Colorado River, no more than a thread of darkness against the coloured rocks.

Did Grandfather really live down there? It looked barbaric, lost and forgotten. Tessa began to feel a qualm of uncertainty. How could she ever hope to find him, without a guide to lead her through those twisting labyrinths? The map she had brought, with its few trails marked, seemed hopelessly inadequate.

'So here you are!'

Spinning round, Tessa gasped and then groaned. Behind her, dark eyes inimical, mouth set in exasperated lines, was Crane Mellor. He stood with insolent ease, hands in the pockets of his jeans, relaxed yet watchful.

'What are you doing here?' Tessa demanded, recovering her breath.

'What are *you*?' Crane stepped forward. 'Come to admire the view? It's quite something, isn't it? Or—were you maybe planning to run away?'

'Run away? I'm sorry, I don't know what you mean.' Tessa was uncomfortably aware of the glances of other people, but she kept her voice cool. 'I've nothing—nobody—to run away from.'

'No, maybe not, but you were planning an escape all the same.' His eyes flickered, almost as if he was laughing at her. 'Or why would you have asked Emery to show you where Grandpa lives, and then come straight out here?' He moved a little closer, took hold of her arm with one long-fingered hand and said silkily, 'Maybe you were planning on visiting Grandpa all by yourself—without waiting for me.'

'And what if I was?' Tessa snapped. 'As I said before, there's no reason at all why I shouldn't, and if I choose——'

'No reason?' Quickly, Crane twisted her around so that she was once more looking out over the depths of the Canyon. 'Look at that, Tessa, and use your sense. You can't possibly go down there on your own, without the faintest idea of what the Canyon's like inside. You don't know what precautions to take, how far it is—anything.' His fingers were cruel on her arm as he dragged her back and began to march her away from the Rim and the photographing tourists. 'You're just acting plain plumb crazy, and it's as well Emery told me what you were up to the minute I got back from my flight. If you'd tried to go down there alone—especially at this time of day, with only a few hours to sunset—well, God knows what might have happened to you.' They were back at his car now, Tessa struggling helplessly in his grip, and he opened the door and thrust her inside. 'Now, let's have no more of these teenage hysterics,' he said grimly, fastening her into her seat-belt before he went round the car to get in his own side. 'I told you, you wait until I'm good and ready to take you, and if that's not fast enough for you, I'm sorry but that's the way it is. Now, d'you understand that?'

Reluctantly, Tessa nodded. Her glimpse of the Canyon had been enough to show her that it wasn't a trip to undertake alone. Until then, she still hadn't fully realised its sheer immensity, or its savage wildness. Clearly, however much she disliked the idea, she was going to have to wait for Crane to take her.

And she might as well do it with good grace, she decided, feeling slightly ashamed of her behaviour. After all, he'd been pretty helpful really—meeting her at Las Vegas, having her to stay in his house. He couldn't have done much more.

It was just that he was so damned overbearing, and cynical. And—she had to admit it to herself, though she never would to him—so overwhelmingly attractive.

Tessa stole a look at his profile and sighed. In other circumstances, she might have . . . But it wasn't any good thinking that way. Because Crane had shown her quite clearly how *he* felt. And now that he knew how she responded to his kisses—even now, her skin burned at the memory—she was going to have to be doubly careful.

'Can you ride?'

Crane asked the question abruptly, jerking Tessa out of her thoughts. She had been surprised to find him at breakfast this morning instead of already at the airfield, and she certainly hadn't expected anything so civilised as conversation.

'I can a bit,' she answered cautiously. 'I used to go and help out at the local riding-stables at home, when I was about twelve or thirteen.' There had been three of them, all pony-mad youngsters whose parents hadn't been able to afford their own ponies, or even regular lessons, and they had worked long and willingly at all the least desirable chores of the stable in return for the occasional ride.

Crane grunted. 'You'll find this a bit different from polite rides round the English countryside,' he said disparagingly. 'Still, I guess it's better than nothing.'

Tessa stared at him. What on earth was he talking

about? She hadn't come here to play cowboys.

'You don't have to entertain me,' she told him coolly. 'As you very well know, I came to see my grandfather, and all I'm asking is that you should take me to him. I don't have to be taken on picnics like a child.'

Crane gave a bark of laughter. 'Picnics! What we'll be doing won't be any picnic, I can tell you that.' He got up from the table and walked with an easy, loping stride to the door. Tessa scrambled to her feet too—he'd avoided her too much in the past few days, and she wasn't going to let him get away again.

'Look, you don't have to worry about me getting bored,' she said with some sarcasm, certain that Crane Mellor wasn't worrying about her in any way. 'I told you, I don't need entertaining—I just want to see my grandfather. And I'd like to see him soon. I can understand your not wanting me here—*I* don't want to be here—so why on earth don't you take me to wherever it is he lives? And then you can forget all about me.'

She was between Crane and the door now, feet planted firmly on the floor, head back so that she could look straight up into those dark, satanic eyes. There was a gleam in them now that scared her a little, but she tilted her head back a little more, determined not to let him see it. All right, so he was annoyed—well, he'd annoyed her too!

Crane stared down at her. His mouth was grim in his lean face and she saw a small muscle twitch in his cheek before he answered. When he spoke, his voice was controlled, but she could sense the anger underneath as if it were a chained tiger waiting to be unleashed.

'Let's get this straight, little cousin,' he said slowly, as if measuring each word. 'Like I said before, nobody invited you here. You came of your own accord. So it's not exactly fair to expect me or anyone else to drop everything just to suit your convenience. You just have to wait around until I can spare the time for the trip—right?' He paused, his eyes moving slowly over her face. 'As it happens, I've been working all the hours God sent during the past few days so that I can take a bit of time off to take you to Grandpa. That's why I asked you if you could ride—we go by mule. And we'll be leaving in——' he glanced at his watch '—a little under an hour. So if you wouldn't mind getting your things together—you'll need enough for a few days, but we travel light, no frilly frocks or suchlike—we can be on our way. That suit you?'

He didn't wait for an answer but put Tessa aside as if she had been a piece of furniture and shouldered his way through the door, leaving her standing breathless in the big, sunny kitchen. Opening her mouth to retort, she turned after him—but the door swung shut in her face and she was alone.

Tessa sank back on her stool. The cheek of the man! Telling her to be ready, just like that—and telling her they were going by *mule*, of all things, without even asking if she wanted to! As it happened, she didn't want to—not in the least. Mules, she'd heard, were awkward, recalcitrant animals, and horribly uncomfortable to ride. Perhaps that's why he'd chosen them as transport—just to make things worse for her.

And the fact that he'd apparently been working overtime in order to make the trip didn't help at all. It put her under an obligation, and that was definitely something she didn't want. If only she'd known what he was doing, it wouldn't have been so bad—but to fling it in her face when she'd just been haranguing him over his *lack* of co-operation—oh, it was too bad!

Still, the main thing was that he was actually taking her to see her grandfather—that soon she would be able to talk to the old man who had been so much in her mother's thoughts, and maybe even win him over. Not that she really thought there was much chance of that—you couldn't break twenty-five years of angry silence with a word—but if she could just be around for a while, show him that an English granddaughter wasn't such a bad thing after all, well, it might work. And at least she would have tried.

Just under an hour, Crane had said! Tessa jumped up and hurried from the kitchen to her own room. She hadn't got long to decide what to take and what to leave behind, if she were to be ready in time. And she didn't want to start off on the wrong foot by keeping him waiting.

During the drive to the Rim, Crane broke his silence to tell Tessa what he intended to do. The mules were located at the top of the Bright Angel trail—one of the steep, twisting paths that descended to the Canyon floor—and although most of them were used for daily rides for visitors, Crane had arranged for two to be kept back.

'We'll go down the Bright Angel trail ourselves,' he said. 'And then we'll need to stay overnight before we go the rest of the way to Grandpa's. So I hope you're ready for a strenuous time.' From the glance he gave her, Tessa knew that he doubted it, and she made up her mind to prove him wrong.

'I'm tougher than I look,' she said lightly, thinking of the hectic games of squash and badminton she played at home, and the long hours of swimming which was her favourite recreation. 'Anyway, I assume I'll be doing no more than thousands of visitors do.'

Crane shrugged. 'Could be. But don't forget, those visitors are generally pretty tough youngsters, used to hiking and backpacking. The ones who just come to gawp do it from the Rim—or maybe they walk a little way down one of the trails and then turn round and come back. It's a long, long way down there—and it can seem even further to come back.'

Tessa understood why when she stood again at the Rim and stared out over the silent, brooding mountains that stretched away in front of her, and below. Their strange, exotic shapes reminded her of pictures she had seen of the great sacred buildings of India and the Far East. It was difficult to believe that such spectacular shapes could have been sculpted by nature.

Crane parked the station wagon at the El Tovar Hotel, a long, impressive building only three storeys high, perched on the very edge of the Rim. He led the way inside. 'We'll have some coffee in the Rendezvous before we start the trip.'

Tessa looked around her, impressed by the big, almost square lounge with its dark-stained log walls and thick, beamy rafters. Low, comfortable-looking chairs and sofas were dotted about and she sank into one as a pleasant-faced waitress, wearing an oddly old-fashioned uniform of high-necked black dress covered by a stiff white pinafore, came forward to take their order.

'Hi, Liza,' Crane said easily, giving her the smile that so transformed his face, and that he so rarely gave Tessa. 'So we're to have special treatment today, are we?'

'Since it's you, and the other girls happen to be busy right now,' the waitress said, and smiled at Tessa. 'So you're Crane's cousin from England—glad to know you. Have you learned to keep him in order yet?'

Crane laughed outright at this, and Tessa felt the colour come into her face. Obviously, he wasn't so dour with everyone else as he was with her!

'Not yet,' she said, keeping her voice light, 'but I shouldn't think that's a very easy task anyway, is it? Perhaps I should take lessons.'

'Oh, don't come to me!' the other girl laughed. 'Anyway, it should be easy for you—you're family. Coffee for both of you?' She nodded, laughing again, brought them their coffee and went away.

Family, Tessa thought, feeling suddenly bleak and lonely. Was that really how people saw her and Crane—as family? She had never felt less close to anyone.

'You're honoured,' Crane observed, leaning back in his chair and stretching out his long legs. 'Liza isn't really a waitress—she gives historical tours of the hotel, wearing the Harvey Girl uniform to make it more authentic. She conducts them as if it were really back in 1910—does it very well, too.'

Tessa looked at him in surprise. 'Historical tours?'

'That's right.' He slanted a quizzical glance at her. 'England's not the only place with a history—I guess ours is a little more recent, but it means a lot to us just the same. The El Tovar has quite a story.' He leaned forward and stirred his coffee. His eyes were abstracted. 'It was still pretty new—just seven years old—when Grandpa was born. Built by a man called Fred Harvey. And the girl he married—your grandmother—was one of the Harvey girls.'

'The Harvey girls? You mean a daughter—no, grand-daughter, surely—of Fred Harvey?'

Crane laughed. 'No, she was no relation to old Fred. The Harvey girls were the young women who worked at his hotels. They were brought out here to cook and clean and wait at table, and they all signed an agreement that they would stay on at the hotel for at least a year, and not get married during that time.'

'And they agreed to that?' Tessa's voice was indignant.

'They did, and why not? Fred had paid their travelling expenses, bought them decent clothes. Naturally, a lot of them didn't keep to that agreement.' Crane's voice seemed to imply that it was unreasonable to expect any woman to keep to an agreement. 'They came out West looking for adventure and romance, and once they found it, they took it. More than twenty thousand of them married—ranchers, cowboys, railroad workers, miners . . . there weren't that many women out here in those days. I reckon Fred Harvey would have done well to run an official marriage bureau alongside his hotels. He was doing a public service, bringing all those women out here.'

Tessa bit back her words, hardly knowing what to object to most: the idea of girls agreeing to sign away their private lives and rights, or the attitude implicit in Crane's words that they were little more than 'marriage-fodder'. All the same, she couldn't help picturing the romantic side of those days—girls coming out almost as pioneers to a part of the country that was still virtually frontier land, arriving among this spectacular scenery to be wooed and courted by men who lived tough lives, carving out railroads, hunting for gold, riding for days on end across vast cattle ranges ... No wonder so many of the girls broke their contracts!

'Harvey wouldn't take just any girl,' Liza said, coming back with more coffee. 'The girls had to be of good character, attractive and intelligent—so it was no wonder that the men wanted to marry them.'

'And although they broke their contracts, they obviously thought a lot of old Fred Harvey,' Crane broke in with another grin. 'There are still plenty of old men around, born at the turn of the century or soon afterwards, called either Fred or Harvey! I reckon he did the West quite a service, in his way. Brought out the kind of woman who made a good pioneering wife.'

'And understood the social graces as well,' Liza added. 'Those Harvey girls founded quite a lot of the first families in the West, and what they'd learned as Harvey girls kept standards up when they might well have dipped right down. Kept you men on your toes!'

Crane laughed and Tessa watched him, wondering. He seemed quite a different person here, with someone he evidently knew well and felt at ease with—pleasant, easy-going, good-humoured. She wished suddenly that he could be this way with her. But there was little chance; as she'd thought before, he'd been poisoned by the bitterness of his grandfather.

And if Crane, who had been only a boy when her mother had left, could be so bitter towards her, was there any chance that her grandfather would be any easier to win round?

Tessa was almost sorry to leave the rustic elegance of the El Tovar, but as they came outside again and the heat struck at her face, she began to feel that at last she was on her way. Up till now, the trip had been a mere preparation—now she was beginning the last, exciting stage of her journey to meet her grandfather and put right the wrongs of a quarter of a century.

All the same, when they arrived at the corral at the edge of the Rim, she approached the mules gingerly, looking at their bony backs and long ears. Was she really supposed to ride down that steep, winding trail on one of these? And what about her luggage?

'That'll all go in the panniers,' Crane said tersely. He took the bag she had packed and began to empty it. 'What in hell's name have you got here? I thought I told you to travel light.'

'So I did!' Tessa reached forward and snatched the bag away before he could drag all her spare shorts, shirts and underwear out to the public gaze—not that there were many people about now, only a few sightseers and the teenage boy who had been waiting with the mules. 'Look, I can pack it, thank you very much—where does it have to go, into this pannier?'

'That's right.' He stood back and watched sardonically while Tessa, her face burning, tried to transfer pants and bras from one bag to another without their being seen. Then she took herself to task. What on earth was the matter with her? She was a woman, wasn't she? Crane knew that, and presumably he knew that women wore underclothes— they were nothing to be ashamed of. With an impatient flick, she pulled out her flimsiest bra and shook it out, re-folding it with exaggerated care.

'There, it's all gone in quite easily,' she said at last, buckling up the strap. 'What goes in the other side?'

'Food and water,' Crane said laconically. 'Mostly water.'

He produced a plastic container that must have held at least a gallon, and handed it to her.

'Good heavens,' she said, 'is that for both of us?'

'No, that's yours. And don't imagine it's any more than you'll need—we have more problems in the Canyon with folk who don't carry enough water than anything else. It's twenty degrees hotter down there than it is on the Rim, and it's pretty rough going whether you're hiking or on mules. And speaking of mules—have you ever had to deal with one before?'

Tessa shook her head. 'I told you, I used to help at——'

'Yeah, I remember, the polite English ponies. Well, you'll find these a mite different. They're sure-footed and know the trail—but you can't take liberties with them. And they're funny about people—they're scared of sudden movements or noises. So if we pass any hikers, take a lot of care. Even someone just dropping a sweater or shouting out can set a mule off, and those trails aren't wide. Think you can cope?'

'I don't seem to have much choice, do I?' Tessa said crossly. In fact, she would far rather have walked down the trail than mount the rangy, long-eared beast now regarding her with such deep suspicion, but she wasn't going to tell Crane that. He'd already made it clear that he thought she was a liability on a trip such as this. It wouldn't take much, she suspected, for him to call the whole thing off—and that was something she was determined not to risk.

Grimly, she mounted and settled herself on the mule's back. The saddle was different from any she had used before and felt uncomfortable, but she was conscious of Crane's eyes on her and said nothing. She gathered up the reins and leaned forward to pat the mule between the ears.

'Do they have names?' she enquired casually, glancing round at the attendant.

'Yours is Bruno, his is Curly,' the boy answered. 'You won't have any trouble with them, I guess. It's pretty quiet on the trail today—the real busy season hasn't started yet, and the main string went down over an hour ago. You might meet some of them coming back from Plateau Point.'

'That's a shorter ride,' Crane told Tessa as they rode bumpily away from the corral. 'A lot of people hike there or take mules, for the view of the Canyon. It's different wherever you go, and even a short way down inside you get a completely different perspective.'

Perched uncomfortably on her mule, Tessa wondered what it was like on the Canyon floor. Would she feel claustrophobic, hemmed in by the soaring, mile-high walls? Would it be dark and sombre down there, shadowed from the sun? And why had her grandfather chosen to live there, far away from the civilisation of the 'outside'?

Crane had steadfastly refused to discuss the old man, or even to describe where he lived. 'You'll find out soon enough,' was all he would say, and Tessa had been forced to wait. Well, she wouldn't have to wait much longer. They were almost at the head of the trail, about to begin the steep descent into the Canyon itself.

Afterwards, Tessa went over that trip in her mind, almost unable to believe that she had accomplished it. The trail had been steeper than she had expected, looking even worse from the back of a mule. She felt acutely vulnerable perched up there, his back making a disturbingly steep downward slope of its own, so that when Tessa looked between his long ears she could see a terrifying drop with the path zigzagging away almost vertically until it disappeared from sight. Why, he's only got to shrug his shoulders and I'd be off, she thought nervously. And what if some hikers pass us who don't know about mules being nervous . . .? She glanced up as Crane turned to look back at her, and wanted to tell him she'd changed her mind and would walk down. But the ironic twist to his mouth was so annoying that she merely bit her lip before giving him a bright smile and assuring him that she was fine.

After a while, however, she grew accustomed to the odd, rocky motion and even to the frightening vistas that fell away below her. She began to look around. Crane had been right—once inside the Canyon, you did get a different perspective, and as they dropped lower and lower she gazed in awe at the soaring cliffs, the huge *mesas* and *buttes* that came into sight as the view slowly unfolded.

'What do you think of it then?' Crane asked when they stopped at a wide spot to give the mules a rest and take a drink of water from the canteens. 'Glad you came?'

Tessa looked at him. There was no trace of irony in his voice, nor in his face, and he seemed genuinely interested in her reaction. She sensed his pride in the spectacular scenery which was his home, and had no wish to deflate it.

'It's the most wonderful place I've ever seen,' she said quietly. 'I can understand anyone wanting to spend a lifetime here. It seems that the more you discover, the more there is to discover. And it's so vast—could anyone *ever* discover all its secrets?'

'I guess not,' he said thoughtfully. 'And that just makes it even more special, hm?'

'Yes, it does. A wilderness that can never be tamed.' Tessa drank some water, grateful for its refreshing coolness.

'It's the colour I really can't get over. There's so much of it! Red—cream—grey—yellow—black—all the bands of colour that tell you about the millions of years that have gone by.' She stared around at the turreted hills, the spires of rock. 'Does anybody really know how it was formed?'

'Not really. There are various theories, but no one knows for certain.' Crane stood up and stretched. 'And that's the way it should be. The Canyon's bigger than man. It can teach us a lot—but we shouldn't expect it to give up all its knowledge.' His dark eyes glinted down at her. 'We'd better be getting along. We've still got a long way to go.'

Tessa climbed back on to her mule, wondering if she would ever get used to the long, lumpy spine. So far they had had no trouble with the animals, and she was feeling a little less vulnerable as they bumped down the stony track. It was early yet to meet hikers coming up, Crane had told her; most of them starting on the nine-hour trek up the trail would be reaching this point about mid-afternoon. They could expect to meet the first ones at midday, or thereabouts.

In fact, they were sitting on a rock and eating their lunch when the first perspiring hikers straggled past them. Tessa looked at their hot faces and damp hair, and thought ruefully of her return journey. Presumably it would be made by mule, but was that really going to be any more comfortable, perched on that hard back which would then be permanently uphill instead of down? That was the big snag of the Grand Canyon—at least, if you climbed a mountain, you got the hard part over first!

It was four o'clock when they finally reached the floor of the Canyon. Tessa eased her back in relief as she felt the mule's body straighten out on the level ground, and twisted her head around to stare up at the rearing cliffs all around them. Down here, it was impossible to imagine a world beyond those soaring towers. Had she really come down so far—had she really ever been so high? Awed, she gazed at the remote plateaux so far above and pictured the people up there, getting out of cars and coaches, exclaiming to each other and clicking away with their cameras. Was that the real world?

Or was it here, in this deep, quiet valley where only the river moved quickly, where the air was clear and unpolluted, and where the only sounds were natural ones— a steady fall of water flowing in a spring from the limestone wall and cascading down to a clear blue pool, the call of a bird from a nearby bush, a rustle of some small animal in the undergrowth . . .?

'We'll get off and walk here for a bit,' Crane said, swinging easily from his saddle. 'Give the mules a break, and stop you stiffening up too much.'

'And you wouldn't, of course,' Tessa said, following his example. 'Sitting in an aeroplane all day is better preparation for mule-riding than anything *I'm* likely to have done, back in England.'

Crane grinned at her. 'You've got it,' he said cheerfully, and Tess felt ashamed of her cattiness. This wasn't the place for bickering, anyway. She felt the calm peace of the Canyon pervade her soul. Maybe she and Crane could be friends. She gave him a tentative smile and was rewarded by another grin.

Really, he's very attractive, she thought, catching the white flash of his teeth. And when he was talking to Liza he seemed friendly and nice. Couldn't we start again?

Wouldn't it make a difference with their grandfather,

too, if he found them on good terms? Wouldn't it make the purpose of her visit a lot easier to achieve?

Tessa gave her mule a pat on the nose and gathered his reins in one hand to lead him along the track behind Crane. She still didn't think she could ever really *like* her American cousin—he was too different from anyone she had ever known before, too tough and aggressive, not her type at all. But if she could dispel the antagonism that she'd sensed at their first meeting, it could certainly make things more comfortable.

And once this part of her trip was over, once she had met and—hopefully—made friends with her grandfather, she could go away and start enjoying herself. She could forget Crane Mellor and the strange, enigmatic glance he kept giving her; forget the tingling in her spine when he looked at her, and the twitch of excitement in her stomach whenever they accidentally touched.

They were sensations she didn't much like and hadn't even acknowledged until now. The sooner she could forget them, the better.

CHAPTER THREE

'You mean we've got to sleep the night *here*? On the bare ground?'

Tessa stared at the grassy hollow, then at Crane. He was standing casually by his mule, his hand resting lightly on its neck, but she sensed a tension in him that he was trying not to show. His dark brows twitched and she caught a gleam in his eye.

'You got it,' he said laconically. 'What's the matter? Don't you ever sleep out under the stars, back in—where is it—Sussex County?'

'We don't call it that,' Tessa said tersely. 'Just Sussex . . . And no, we don't sleep out under the stars there. We camp sometimes——' though in fact she had only once camped, with the Girl Guides, '—but when we do that we use tents.'

'Do you, now? Well, I guess with all that rain you'd need 'em.' He was laughing at her, she was sure of it. 'We don't get a lot of rain here in the Canyon in midsummer,' he went on, unbuckling his panniers. 'And when we do it's soon over—though you do have to be careful of flash floods. And there's enough gear to carry, without adding tents to the load. Here——' He threw her a rolled-up package which seemed to fling itself open to reveal a thin, crinkled mattress. 'You'll find that's pretty comfortable. There's a sleeping bag to go with it. That's all you'll need, I reckon.'

Tessa stared at the mattress and sleeping-bag, and then looked a little desperately at her surroundings. In other circumstances, she thought, she could have enjoyed this. There was an element of adventure in it that appealed to her—after all, with her mother's illness and her own education and career to work for, she'd never had much time for the kind of activity holidays some of her friends had talked about. And it certainly was beautiful down here. But with Crane . . .?

Forget it's him, she told herself, laying the bag carefully on top of the mattress. Pretend you're with someone else; someone you like . . .

She walked a little way away from where Crane was setting up camp, and sat down on a rock. She had to hand it to him for knowing the right place to choose, and she wondered if he'd been here before. Well, presumably he must have, on previous visits to Todd. She kept forgetting that Crane looked on Todd as his grandfather too.

They had walked for some distance on the Canyon floor before Crane had turned off the main track. Tessa had been expecting to go to one of the lodges—Phantom Ranch, perhaps—or the camping grounds at Bright Angel or Indian Gardens which Crane had told her about. But apparently Todd didn't live anywhere near these, and the obviously less well-trodden track took them deep among the trees and bushes which she had been surprised to find on the Canyon floor.

'Oh sure, there's plenty of wildlife down here,' Crane said when she remarked on this. 'Plants *and* animals. On the Rim you get the ponderosa pines, the junipers and the desert plants—yucca, prickly pear, saguaro cacti and so on. You get some of them down here too—we passed some good specimens of ocotillo on the way down—but you also get the more lush trees, the oak and maple and aspen.'

'And animals?' Tessa prompted him as he paused to let his mule negotiate a rocky part of the trail.

'Oh, sure. Prairie dog, coyote, bighorn sheep—they're rare now and the rangers like to know if you spot one. Jackrabbits, of course—jaguar——'

'*Jaguar?*' Involuntarily, Tessa glanced over her shoulder. 'Isn't that a kind of lion?'

'Mountain lion, yes.' Crane's mouth twitched. 'No need to look so nervous, little English cousin. You're not likely to be attacked—they're shy animals, don't come near where there might be people. You ought to watch out for rattlesnakes, though.'

With a tremendous effort, Tessa stopped herself looking round again. She had an idea she was providing Crane with quite a lot of amusement. All the same, she felt as if she had grown eyes in her ankles and would have gladly got back on her mule at that point. But Crane was walking ahead again, looking quite unconcerned, so she bit her lip and followed him. He was probably exaggerating the dangers, anyway.

Well, she hoped he was, she thought now, sitting on her rock. Delectable though this place might be, it would soon lose its attractions if it became overrun with mountain lions and rattlesnakes . . .

Tessa lifted her head and looked around the narrow cleft where Crane had decided to stop. She hadn't liked it much as they entered the gloomy chasm, its walls dark and forbidding, and had wondered where Crane might be leading her. But then it had widened into a broad, grassy space and she couldn't repress a gasp of delight.

The delight was still with her. The canyon was like a small amphitheatre, its rocky sides no longer forbidding but glowing with colour. At the end, a spring had forced its way through the pale cream of the limestone and was falling a distance of about thirty feet, glittering in a few last stray sunbeams that had somehow filtered down into this hidden place. The pool at the bottom was clear, reflecting the delicate green of the bushes that surrounded it, and the grey slabs of rock that bordered it looked smooth and inviting.

A swim would be lovely, Tessa thought longingly, and then remembered that she hadn't packed her swimsuit.

Damn! Crane had told her to bring it too, but she hadn't really expected any chance of swimming—after all, she'd heard that the Colorado River itself, storming its way through the Canyon, was too fast and cold. And she'd packed hurriedly, picking up what came first to hand.

She glanced over her shoulder. Crane was out of sight, no doubt still fussing about with the little stove he'd taken out of his pack. He wouldn't be coming along here to look for her—no doubt he was as glad as she was to be alone for a while. And if she just slipped out of her clothes and had a quick dip . . . the pool was sheltered by the bushes, after all . . .

Within moments, Tessa had done just that. Naked, she left her clothes piled on a smooth, flat rock and ran down to the water's edge. She dipped in a toe; it was deliciously cool. Seconds later, she was completely immersed, splashing and laughing under the sparkling spray of the cascade.

This was wonderful! After the long, uncomfortable ride down the steep trail, constantly expecting the mule to slip on a loose stone or take fright at some sudden noise or movement, with the temperature rising inexorably the deeper they descended, Tessa found the peace of the little dell and the coolness of the splashing cascade a balm to her weary body and jaded mind. She swam with lazy strokes across the pool, turning on her back to float, face upturned to the last glimmers of the afternoon sun. The water was as clear as glass, the pebbles at the bottom flickering with colour. Her limbs looked slender and golden as the spray from the waterfall rippled over them, and she stretched her body out on the surface, closing her eyes in sheer bliss.

'Say! Now that *is* a pretty sight!'

Tessa jerked around in the water, losing her balance on the shingly bottom as she did so. Her foot slipped and she found herself under the water, splashing furiously to regain the air, coming up to shake spray from her hair and eyes, dazed and startled.

Crane was standing at the water's edge. And one glance was enough to tell her that he was as naked as she; enough, too, to show her that his lean, long-limbed body was tanned a deep, even brown and as firmly muscled and gracefully virile as any Greek statue.

'Oh!' Burning with embarrassment, Tessa turned away, wondering just how much of her he could see through the clear water. Fortunately, her splashing had created quite a lot of foam, which she hoped was hiding her, but she couldn't keep on thrashing about like a frightened dolphin! And when she risked a quick peep over her shoulder, she could see that he didn't appear to have any intention of moving.

'I didn't think you'd be down here,' she said accusingly, keeping her back to him.

'Snap! And I certainly didn't expect my prim little English cousin to be quite so uninhibited.' His voice was slow, amused. 'Turn around, Tessa. Don't be so embarrassed. We're family, after all.'

Family! Tessa had never felt much kinship with this tall, arrogant American and she felt even less now. Why didn't he just go away, for heaven's sake? Then she could get out and dress, and he could have his own swim.

A sudden splash and surge of water against her face told her that Crane wasn't going away, and he wasn't waiting for his swim. He was in there with her, sharing the pool which suddenly seemed cramped and tiny ... Dismayed, she turned and saw him forging across the pool towards her, his strokes so powerful that only a few were needed to bring him right alongside.

'Crane, no!' Tessa hardly knew what she was saying as she twisted frantically away from him, terrified that he was going to touch her. But there was no way of escape. Behind her, the rocky walls of the canyon rose sheer from the pool, and to reach the tiny, sandy beach or the flat slabs where she had slid into the water, she would have had to push past him—and that, she couldn't do. She backed away from him, then realised that as the water grew shallower she lost its blurring camouflage, and ended in a crouching position, looking up at him like a cornered animal.

'Well, there's no need to look so scared,' he drawled, looming over her. He was standing waist-deep, and her eyes were drawn in fascination to the movement of the muscles under his gleaming brown skin. 'What do you think I'm going to do to you, little English cousin?'

'Oh, I wish you wouldn't call me that!' Tessa snapped, grabbing at this as a chance to release some of her tension.

'Do I call you "big American cousin" all the time?'

'No, but I guess you could if you wanted to.' His amused tone irritated her even more, but at least that was better than being scared. And why *was* she so scared, anyway? So they were both naked, did it really have to make any difference?

No, it didn't *have* to—but it did, all the same, and Tessa didn't want to think about why. She stared up at Crane, trying to keep her eyes on his face and finding it not very easy. He was certainly magnificent, standing there in the green water of the pool, with the cascade falling behind him and the water sparkling on his body ... She realised that he was looking at her with frank appreciation, and also that now the water had settled down again its clarity was providing her with no concealment at all.

'Please,' she said, her voice trembling a little, 'let me get out and then you can have your swim.'

Her heart was thumping, and her knees felt weak. It was the cold of the water, she thought. If only she could get out ... She raised her eyes again and this time met his glance, and her heartbeat seemed to pause momentarily and then jerk against her breast.

Crane's eyes were almost black, the pupils wide against a narrow brown rim. His chest rose and fell quickly, and he reached out a strong, lean hand and touched Tessa's cheek.

'You know,' he said quietly, 'there's something about the Grand Canyon. It can help you to discover yourself—and it can help other people to discover you, too. I reckon we're both going to do a bit of discovering on this trip ... don't you?'

And as Tessa gazed wordlessly up at him, he drew her close to him through the sparkling water. She felt the strength of his arm and hand, curving round her head, the power of his other arm as it half lifted her from the water to hold her against him. She felt the hardness of his body, wet against hers, the rugged outlines of his muscles against her softness. And finally, as she opened her mouth in speechless protest, she felt his lips against hers.

The roaring of the waterfall melted with the roaring of her blood, and the walls of the Canyon reeled above her, tree and sky and rock wheeling through space as Crane's mouth took possession of her, his lips moulding hers, his tongue flicking against her teeth. Tessa felt the gasp shudder through her as she clung to him, unaware that her hand had crept up to tangle in his thick black hair, conscious only of a wild clamour that shook her whole body, of a fierce compulsion that had to be obeyed.

The water was like cool silk, as sensuous as the twining movements her body was making without any apparent direction from her. Vaguely, she knew that this was something completely outside her experience, that she had never known anything like this slow, voluptuous smouldering that was going on inside her, that no watery cascade could ever quench. And although her heart beat as much from fear as from delight, the two were inextricably and pleasurably combined, and she sought Crane's lips again with her own. As Tessa opened her eyes in languorous supplication, he began to withdraw himself from her clinging arms.

'Tessa—*Tessa!*' he muttered, and then, as if he had been stung, he jerked away, letting her fall back into the water and flinging himself backwards to kick away across the pool.

Startled, shaken, Tessa lay in the water, half blinded by

the spray from his vigorous thrusting movements. Her heart was still pounding from his kiss, her body still quivering from his touch. She raised a trembling hand and passed it across her face.

Crane was out of the pool and dragging on a pair of shorts and a shirt. He didn't look at her. He turned away and disappeared through the bushes, and Tessa heard him kicking at small stones and rocks as he stormed his way back to the camp.

Slowly, she swam back to the rocks and clambered out. The sun had disappeared and she was shivering. She looked ruefully at her clothes. There was nothing she wanted to do less than pull them over her wet body, but she had no choice—she hadn't brought a towel to the pool, and she certainly wasn't going to go and fetch one. But even as she reached for them, a towel flew through the air and landed a yard or so away.

'It's all right,' Crane's voice said brusquely. 'I'm not watching you . . . You'd better get yourself dry and dressed as quickly as you can. There'll be a hot drink waiting for you when you want it.' She heard the sounds of his departure again, noisier, she guessed than they needed to be—Crane could, and generally did, move as silently as a cat.

Tessa dried herself hastily and hurried back into her clothes. Her heart was still kicking inside her, and her body quivered when she thought of that brief encounter in the pool. What did it mean? But she knew the answer to that one, she thought bitterly. Nothing more than that Crane was an inveterate womaniser who never missed an opportunity. Thank goodness he'd come to his senses fairly quickly. She hoped he wouldn't forget himself again.

It was her own reaction that worried her more. She'd never responded like that in her life, to any man. And now—twice in only a few days ...

But then, none of her boyfriends had ever kissed her like that, had they? Never held her in quite that way, never transmitted quite such urgency so that her body seemed to catch fire, clamour for more kisses, more caresses, for everything ...

Tessa's cheeks burned. If that was the effect the Grand Canyon was going to have on her, the sooner she was out of it, the better.

Going back to the spot where Crane had chosen to camp was about as easy as entering a tiger's lair, but Tessa knew she had to do it, and when she walked back through the bushes her head was high and her eyes glittering danger. Just let him try anything on again ...! She had recovered from her first shock now and had deliberately fanned her smouldering anger, so that it was ready to flame at the slightest provocation.

Crane was busy with a small stove which he had taken from his capacious panniers along with the other camping gear.

'Why not light a fire?' Tessa asked, her voice tight, but determined to remain as coolly detached as possible. She wasn't going to let him have any suspicion that he might have upset her in any way.

'Because fires aren't allowed in the Canyon.' He didn't bother to look up, simply adjusted the flame and set a pan on top. 'Can't you imagine the damage they'd do down here?'

Tessa felt rebuffed. Of course, it made sense—but did he have to speak to her as if she were a child?

'But I saw some smoke when we were on the way down,' she said, feeling a sudden twinge of panic. 'Something was on fire then—what happens if it spreads? Can we get caught?'

'We could.' His voice was as laconic as ever. 'But it isn't likely, provided nobody's been playing fool tricks with matches.' He lifted the lid and stirred inside the pan, then stood up, towering over her so that she backed away involuntarily. Did he have to stand so close? 'There's a pretty well-organised fire management programme down here,' he went on, his eyes like agate in the tanned face. 'Fire's important—some plants depend on it for their natural cycle and it also releases nutrients stored in dead matter. It clears the undergrowth and lets light in for young plants to grow. So the Park authorities generally allow natural fires to burn. They even set prescribed fires where there's too much litter—I mean natural litter, like dead trees and fallen branches and such. Ground fuel, it's called, and if there's too much you'll get fire all right, but it'll be too intense and do real damage.' He was still standing close, his eyes burning with fires of their own, and although Tessa wanted to move away again, her body refused to stir. 'So all fire is under the control of the authorities, and a blaze started down here by campers could wreck a lot of careful management.'

'Yes, I see,' Tessa said faintly. His nearness was overpowering and she felt weak, dizzy. What had happened to her anger, that she'd put on like a protective cloak? She looked up at him, seeing something she couldn't fathom in those dark, snapping eyes. Crane . . .

'Tessa,' he said quietly. He put out a hand and touched her arm. 'What happened back there—I——'

But Tessa wasn't listening. His touch stung her arm and throbbed through her body like the shock from a bare electrical wire. Jerking away, she felt her anger flood back, and welcomed it with relief.

'Leave me alone!' she exclaimed, leaping back out of his reach. 'Don't you dare touch me again!' Her eyes flashed in the gathering darkness and she thought briefly of the sunset happening overhead, the crowds of people up on the Rim, watching and photographing it. It seemed very lonely down here in the Canyon. 'I don't know what you think I am,' she went on, more quietly now that she was at a safe distance from him, ready to spring away at his slightest move. 'But whatever it is, you can think again. I'm not in the market for a quick fling with anyone—especially not with you. So keep away from me, Crane Mellor, and get me to my grandfather's house as quickly as possible, all right? That's all I'm asking you do do. If you want entertainment on the way you should have brought a pack of cards.'

Crane stood quite still. It was too dark now to see his expression, but Tessa could guess at the stormy anger tightening his face. Tension crackled between them like lightning playing between the rocky walls. She found herself clenching her fists, almost as if preparing for a physical fight. Well, if it came to it, she thought wryly, there would be no holds barred.

But Crane didn't move. Minutes went by . . . and then she sensed his capitulation. He turned away and the tension slackened.

'All right, Tessa,' he said, 'have it your own way. I just wanted to say—well, it doesn't matter. You're not in a mood to listen, anyway. It's getting dark; I'll light the lamp.'

The mundane chores they carried out during the next half-hour—lighting the lamp, which threw a warm glow over their little camp, preparing the supper, laying out their beds—seemed to distance them from the events by the pool, and Tessa found herself gradually feeling more at ease. Crane made no further attempt to touch her, nor did he refer to the kisses they had shared—or, rather, that he had forced upon her, she amended quickly. By the time they were sitting down, eating the stew he had made, Tessa was surprised to find herself feeling quite companionable.

'The moon's up,' she observed, gazing up at the sky which seemed so much higher from down here between the cliffs. She watched the pale globe as it moved slowly above them, casting shafts of silver light between the dense black shadows. 'It'll be really dark when it disappears,' she added with a tiny shiver.

'Not so dark as you'd think. You see the stars then—great clouds of them, like a sparkling shower that never falls. They seem clearer here than anywhere I've been—I guess because there's no artificial light to dim them, and the walls of the Canyon make a kind of funnel.'

'Like looking up an old chimney,' Tessa agreed. 'They say if you do that you can see stars in daytime, but I've never been able to try it.'

'I guess we don't have that kind of chimney in the States.' Crane paused, then said, 'Tell me about your home, Tessa. What's it like, where you live?'

'Oh, very pretty. Sussex is one of the counties along the south coast, you know, but we don't live right by the sea— we live in a little town called Arundel. It's built by a river and on a hill, and there's a huge castle there—the Duke of Norfolk lives in it.'

'Is that so? What kind of population does the town have?'

Tessa was aware that Americans were interested in population figures—every town had, at its entrance, a board stating how many people lived there. But she had to think quite hard before answering him.

'About two and a half thousand, I should think. It's only a small place.'

'I thought England was really crowded,' Crane said.

'Well, it is—we do have a high population, compared with America. But it isn't crammed full. We don't have your huge deserts or prairies, where nobody lives—but we do have quite big parts of fairly empty countryside, like Dartmoor, and lots in Scotland and Wales—moors and mountains where nobody's ever built more than a shepherd's hut or a row of miners' cottages. Sussex is quite highly populated, but we still have woods and fields and downs—hills—where you can get away from people and be quite alone.'

'And is that what you like?' he asked. 'Being alone?'

'Yes, I think it is. I love Arundel, of course—going shopping down the main street and meeting people I know. But I like to get away—into the park, where there's a wildfowl reserve and you can see a herd of deer if you go quietly, or right up on the South Downs where you can see the sea. It's beautiful up there—so free and wild—and it's nearly always windy.' She smiled reminiscently. 'I was caught in a thunderstorm once up there—not really the safest place to be in a storm, on top of a hill—but it was marvellous watching the lightning flash all around the sky and hearing the crash of the thunder. I loved it.'

'You can get some pretty spectacular electrical storms here too,' Crane remarked, and Tessa looked up at the towering walls and believed him. It could be a frightening place, this Canyon, she reflected. Today it had been smiling, but even so she had been aware of its power slumbering beneath the stillness, like the latent strength of some great beast at rest. When the smiling sun vanished behind threatening cloud and the walls darkened, throwing deep shadows into the chasms and valleys below, the beast could wake with a mighty roar and then any human being, caught in all his puny weakness, would be helpless indeed . . . Tessa shivered. How could anyone live down here all the time?

'Tell me about Grandfather,' she said. 'Where does he live—and why did he choose to live there, so far away from everyone? What does he do?'

Crane didn't answer for a moment, and Tessa thought that perhaps he wasn't going to. But just as she was opening her mouth to repeat her question, he spoke. His voice was thoughtful.

'Do? I guess he doesn't do anything much. Just lives— you know? There doesn't seem to be any need to do much more, down here.'

'You mean there's nothing *to* do,' Tessa said flatly.

'No, I don't mean that at all. Oh, there's nothing of what you might call civilisation down here. No television, no movie shows, no hamburgers or fast food. No automobiles, no restaurants, no take-aways. Down here, you're on your own, fending for yourself. You've no one else to rely on— but no one's making demands on you either.' Crane paused. 'I guess that's what Grandpa likes. He's maybe had enough of people and their demands.'

There was a short silence before Tessa said tightly, 'I suppose you mean my mother.'

Crane turned his head, and in the light of the lamp he had set between them, Tessa saw his eyes glint. 'I didn't say that, Tessa. Sure, she was one of the bad patches in his life, but she wasn't the only one.' He paused again. 'I guess she could have done quite a lot to help him over some of the others if she'd been around, that's all.'

Tessa stared at him. 'What do you mean?'

'You don't know, do you?' His voice was quiet yet oddly harsh, like velvet rubbing softly over craggy rock. 'You really don't know.'

'Since my mother never heard a word from anyone from the day she left, it's hardly likely that I would.' Tessa controlled her voice with some difficulty, remembering the pain her mother had suffered through the long years of rejection. 'She did write, you know. She wrote often, telling her father all that was happening in her life—telling him about me, about Stuart, telling him when Dad died. It was like sending letters into space. I used to wonder why she kept trying. I used to watch her, looking out for the postman, riffling through the letters to see if by any chance there might at last be one from America—and when there never was, I used to hate you—all of you.'

'Your privilege, I guess,' he said coldly.

'Yes, it was my privilege—and my right.' Tessa could hear her voice growing stormy now, but there was nothing she could do about it, nothing she wanted to do about it. It was time someone in this stiff-necked, unforgiving family knew just what they had done. 'But it's not a right I enjoyed much,' she went on bitterly. 'I would have loved a family who was interested in me, who wrote and kept me up-to-date with their own news, who loved me even if I did live on the other side of the world. A family who realised that whatever had happened between them and my mother, it wasn't *my* fault—a family who could forgive and forget, who knew what love meant and——'

'Love!' he cut in. 'There's that word again—the word you fling around like it's confetti, without ever stopping to wonder what it really means. If you did, you'd realise it's responsible for most of the hurting that goes on in the world. Love!' He almost spat the word out.

Tessa stared at him, horrified by the vehemence of his voice. Surely he couldn't mean what he had just said? What could have happened in his life to make him feel this way? How could *anyone* have been hurt so badly as to repudiate love?

Tentatively, she reached out a hand and touched his arm. It was bare, his sleeves rolled up to the elbow, and she felt the flinch of his cool skin and drew her hand back at once. Was she so repulsive to him? And if she was—why that scene in the pool?

'You don't know what you're saying,' she said, her voice trembling a little. 'Love *is* good. How can you say that it's responsible for most of the pain in the world? How can you possibly believe that?'

'Oh, easily,' he retorted with a short laugh. 'Do you want me to list my reasons?' He held up his hands, fingers stretched out, and began counting them off. 'Take your mother. She said she loved her father, right? Yet she up and left him when she was still a girl, went off to the other side of the world and never came back. Don't you think that hurt him? He loved her too, but that didn't make any difference. He had to lose her just the same.'

'But that happens,' Tessa said. 'People grow up, fall in

love, leave their parents, all the time. It's a natural part of life.'

'Maybe it is, but that doesn't stop it hurting. And you say it hurt your mother too, so there's some more pain to add to the general burden. Right.' He touched a second finger. 'It didn't stop there, did it? What happened between your mother and her father hurt all the rest of the family. Even me.' He shook his head. 'Still say it's a good thing?'

'But it needn't have done all that,' Tessa insisted. 'If only Grandfather had been able to accept what happened, it needn't have hurt anyone. It's not love that caused all that pain—it's selfishness and jealousy. Can't you see that?'

'All right,' he said, either not hearing her words or ignoring them, 'let's go on. Let's look at what happened after your mother left.'

'After she left? But you've told me——'

'I haven't.' Crane's voice was grim and Tessa felt a sudden pang of fear. What *had* happened after her mother and father had run away to get married?

'It's never occurred to you to ask, has it?' he said, and the coldness in his voice struck Tessa like ice in her heart. 'It's just never occurred to you to wonder where *my* parents fit into all this—where they might be now.'

'*Your* parents?' Tessa stared at him, at the gleam of his eyes shining in the lamplight. She sought for words, but found nothing to say. He was right, she realised with a stab of dismay. She hadn't ever asked—hadn't even wondered. If she'd thought about them at all—Joe and Willa—she would simply have assumed that they'd moved away. But nobody had ever mentioned them, and Tessa had been too disorientated, too jet lagged and bewildered on her arrival, to think straight.

But that wasn't any excuse, she told herself. She *ought* to have thought about them—ought to have asked Crane. They were part of her family too, and it had been inexcusable to forget about them.

'I'm sorry,' she said simply 'I just assumed—well, that they weren't here any more. I suppose I was thinking mostly about Grandfather.'

'Oh, you were right,' he said with an odd note in his voice, a note that made her look at him sharply and catch her breath. 'They're not here any more. They haven't been here for about—oh, let's see—twenty-two or three years.'

'Twenty-two or three . . . but that must be soon after my mother left.' Tessa's eyes widened. 'You mean *they* left, too? Left him all alone here? Well, no wonder——'

She didn't finish. Crane cut in, his voice curt, one hand raised as if to stop her words physically.

'No, Tessa, it's not like that. They didn't leave—not in the sense you mean. They died. They were killed in an aircraft accident down in the Canyon. Flying in supplies to some of the people who live down there.' He paused, and to Tessa, too shocked to speak, it seemed as if the whole Canyon held its breath, waiting for his next words. 'That's when Grandpa needed your mother most. When my mum and dad were killed he was left with nothing. Nobody, except me—a boy of thirteen, more liability than help.'

'Oh, God,' Tessa said softly. 'How dreadful—poor Grandfather.' Again, on impulse, she put out her hand and laid her fingers on his arm. 'And you, too—losing your parents like that. Crane, I'm so very, very sorry.'

For a few moments they were silent together, wrapped in a tiny pool of light within the massive darkness of the great Canyon. This time, Crane didn't flinch away from Tessa's hand. But neither did he respond, and she had a strong feeling that he didn't even know it was there, that he was back in some private hell of his own, a hell he had first known when he was only thirteen. But even that wasn't all—Crane had been adopted, and that hinted at another tragedy, back in his early childhood—when he'd lost his original parents . . .

Was it really any wonder that he was bitter, afraid to love?

After a few moments, she took her hand away, and then an owl called somewhere and Crane stirred.

'That was when he really needed your mother,' he said again. 'But she wasn't there, was she? She was away on the other side of the world, enjoying *her* idea of love, putting a stranger first, forgetting her own family.'

Tessa was stung to retort.

'That's not fair! She didn't even *know*. If she had, she would have come straight back—of course she would. Joe was her brother! She would have been here at once—but nobody told her. How could that be her fault?'

She bit her lip and wondered yet again whether her mission could have even the faintest chance of success. If this was the way Crane felt . . . how could she expect any response at all from her grandfather?

'Look, it's time we turned in,' Crane said, breaking a silence that had gone on too long. 'Talking like this does no good, just rakes up old badness . . . OK, so you had to know, but now let's leave it at that. I've laid your bedroll out here, not too close to mine. I didn't reckon you'd be feeling too friendly.'

His tone was sardonic and Tessa flushed, glad of the darkness to hide her colour. She went over to the bed Crane had prepared for her. In spite of his saying it wasn't too close to his, the two sleeping-bags were only a yard apart. But she didn't feel disposed to move hers further away—she had a feeling that here, in this mysterious darkness, she was going to be glad of human contact fairly close. Even if it did have to be Crane.

She looked at the bedroll again. It looked reasonably comfortable, but where was she supposed to undress? She glanced over her shoulder and saw that Crane was already shrugging out of his shirt and unfastening the waistband of his jeans. Quickly, she turned away again.

'It's all right,' he said coolly, from behind her. 'I'm not going to look. Of course, you can sleep in your clothes if you want—it won't bother me either way—but you'll feel more comfortable if you take them off.'

Tessa heard him getting into his sleeping bag and settling down. She risked a quick glance, and saw that he was indeed facing the other way. Rapidly, as if afraid that he might turn his head at any minute—though why it should matter, after that scene in the pool, she hadn't the faintest idea—she dragged off her shirt and jeans and wriggled into her own bag.

'Goodnight,' Crane said, his voice remote.

'Goodnight,' Tessa answered. She lay looking up at the sky, seeing the stars like a cloud of sparkling lights above the Rim of the Canyon. Suddenly, she realised how tired she was, and longed for sleep.

But it didn't come. Long after Crane's breathing had slowed, becoming regular and even, the only sound apart from that of the steady fall of the cascade, she was still lying awake. Still thinking over all that he had told her.

Her uncle and aunt, Joe and Willa, dead since before she

was born ... Crane, orphaned—for the second time, perhaps?—at the age of thirteen ... Her mother, lost on the other side of the world.

What was she going to see when she finally met her grandfather? A bitter man, filled with hatred, who could no longer listen to reason? Or a man broken and destroyed by the harshness of his life, living as a recluse, afraid to make human contact because of the pain that might result?

And Crane, the man who lay beside her, a man in the prime of his life, powerful, vigorous, virile—the colour washed over her again at the memory of his kiss, the way he had held her, the hardness of his body against hers. Would he, too, let bitterness rule his life? Would he, too, end his days alone at the bottom of the world's deepest ravine?

The thought was oddly painful. And once again, Tessa reached out her hand and touched his arm, the arm that lay flung outside the sleeping-bag.

Crane was asleep. He didn't flinch away. But he rolled towards her, and his other hand came over and fastened on hers, holding it there against his skin.

With a tiny sigh, Tessa fell asleep.

CHAPTER FOUR

TESSA stirred, turned over, and stretched. She had been dreaming and she kept her eyes closed, not wanting to wake up and lose the flavour of the dream. It had been happy, filling her with a sense of comfort and delight, a sense that went with the fresh morning air that was gently caressing her face . . .

No, it was gone. Sighing, she opened her eyes.

The walls of the Grand Canyon reared into the sky all around her, clothed with green near the floor, stark red and grey and white as they soared higher. High above, she could see an eagle wheeling; close by, in some bushes, she could hear the twittering of smaller birds. She froze as her eye caught the shimmer of a humming-bird, no bigger than a large dragonfly, its wings vibrating so rapidly that she could see only the shivering brilliance of their turquoise colouring. Tessa lay very still, watching it until at last it flew away.

She turned the other way and found herself gazing into Crane's eyes, only inches away from her own.

They were like tigers' eyes, she thought, dark and brooding and enigmatic. And, like the stone that went by the same name, hard and unyielding. What lay behind them? Bitterness, she knew. But was that really all? There had to be more than that to a man like Crane, a man who ran his own small airline, who chose to stay in the place where he'd been born rather than roam the world looking for a different kind of success. And it had been a deliberate decision, of that she was sure—Crane could have gone anywhere, done anything. So why had he decided to stay here?

Was it because of what had happened to the grandfather they were on their way to meet? Because of her mother's desertion—and his parents' terrible accident?

Or was there something else—something she hadn't yet found out? Something that, perhaps, she would never be told, so that she would never be able to solve the enigma of Crane?

'Awake?' Crane said, and reached out a finger to touch her cheek, smoothing back the tousled hair. 'Sleep all right?' His hard shell of reserve seemed to have disappeared, as if discarded with the clothes that he had taken off the previous night.

'Yes—yes, I did, thanks.' Tessa lay quite still, powerless to move. There was a strange intimacy in being down here with Crane, warm and comfortable in her sleeping-bag, aware of being very nearly naked yet decently covered, with the morning air washing their faces and the rugged cliffs rising high above.

Crane's fingers moved lightly over her skin, as gentle as the breeze as they stroked the curve of her cheek, following it down the line of her slender neck to the pulse that was beating with sudden raggedness in her throat. She felt the kick of her heart against her ribs, the sudden tingling spiral of excitement in her stomach, and caught her breath. She wanted to move, to cover his hand with her own, to push it away—draw it closer . . . her mind in turmoil, she wasn't sure which she wanted most. But the sleeping-bag trapped her, and her limbs felt paralysed.

'Tessa.' His voice was a whisper, and she wasn't even sure that he had spoken. It could have been the zephyr breeze . . . the murmur of the cascade . . . Her eyes wide, imploring, she gazed at him, saw the intention in his face and knew that she couldn't resist.

'Tessa . . .' This time, she saw his lips shape the word and even as she watched them, they moved closer, closer to her own. Helpless, she closed her eyes and felt the soft touch of his mouth against her cheek, her eyelids, stroking down to her neck, discovering that wildly fluttering pulse and teasing it gently before moving up again to possess her own quivering lips. But there was none of the urgent, demanding hardness of the lips that had taken her by storm yesterday; only a tender exploration which softened her protest and had her dizzy in the arms that were now enfolding her. With a tiny moan of acquiescence, she let her head fall back, arching her neck against the hand that caressed it, moving sensuously closer to him. The sleeping-bags were an encumbrance now, she thought dazedly, wanting the hard warmth of his body against hers, and tried to wriggle free.

She felt Crane sigh against her mouth, sensed the withdrawal in him, and sudden panic made her tighten her own arms around him, her mouth seeking his with a desperation she barely understood.

'All right—that's enough.'

The words were quiet, regretful, but they had the effect of stopping Tessa short. Her eyelids flew open and she looked again into Crane's eyes, seeing a different kind of darkness there, a fathomless depth that she wanted with sudden urgency to plumb, knowing instinctively that here was a wealth she could find nowhere else. She found her hands on his shoulders and tightened them on the bare, muscular flesh, trying to pull him closer, wanting to discover fully the knowledge that had come to her in that brief flash of awareness and as quickly departed, leaving her with a sense of irreplaceable loss and a deep, yearning hunger. Her lips parted in longing invitation. She had forgotten everything in the need of the moment, in her need of him.

'Steady, Tessa.' His voice was still gentle, but there was a warning note in it. 'Quieten down now. Don't let's do anything we might regret.'

Regret?

The word hit Tessa like a punch to the heart. Regret—why should they regret, when it all seemed so right, so inevitable? What could there be to regret . . .? And then memory came surging back, the memory of Crane's bitterness, his hostility, of the family history that lay between them. And Tessa felt her body sag in his embrace, felt him lay her gently back and move away, leaving her strangely chilled.

What on earth had possessed her? The faint memory of her dream, whatever it was? The effect of waking here, in this strange, mystic place, so far from any other human being? The mere propinquity of a virile male who was clearly not averse to the odd sexual adventure, in spite of—perhaps even because of—his cynicism above love?

Tessa felt her entire body grow hot, burning with shame, and she turned away.

'Don't let it worry you,' Crane said quietly. 'Just look on it as a good-morning kiss. After all, we *are* cousins—we might as well be kissing-cousins. First thing in the morning, anyway—whatever we feel like later on.'

There was a quiver in his voice which Tessa took to be amusement. It brought back a touch of anger that was a relief, welcome in its familiarity. At least when she was angry with him she knew where she stood! She turned back, looking up to find Crane out of his sleeping-bag and already fastening his jeans.

'I feel no differently towards you than I've ever done,' she said coolly. 'So you're my cousin. Well, since we never had any contact until a week ago, I don't really see why that should make me feel any closer to you than to any other man I've only just met. In which case, we'll leave the kissing bit out of it, if you don't mind, and get on with what I came for—which was to meet my grandfather.'

Crane looked down at her and she saw an odd spark in his eyes. What was it—a glint of laughter, or of something else, something she couldn't analyse? She decided to read it as laughter, and her irritation grew. Just what was he playing at? Had he made that pass at her—because that's what it had been, even if he had called a halt first—just to make her respond, so that he could gain the upper hand? Had he done it solely to humiliate her?

Well, he wouldn't get the chance again!

'Sure, we'll go and meet Grandpa,' Crane said evenly. 'But first—breakfast. I'll go along and wash at the pool, shall I? That'll give you the chance to get dressed in privacy——' again that glint of laughter '—and then while you're having a wash I'll get some food together. And after that, we'll be on our way.' He walked away down the twisting path through the bushes, his lean body moving with loose-limbed ease, his buttocks small and tight in the close-fitting jeans. 'Shan't be long.'

Tessa watched him go. She felt oddly deprived, as though she had lost something valuable. But that was nonsense, she told herself robustly. Crane was nothing to her. She'd known about him ever since she was a child—known of his existence—but until now, he hadn't had any effect on her whatsoever. And it hadn't made any difference, had it?

All the same, she had a feeling that the last few days had brought something extra into her life, some new dimension, an element that hadn't been there before. Something that, if lost, would leave her world strangely empty.

For the rest of that morning, they said very little. Crane came back from the pool and Tessa went for her own wash—though this time she didn't strip and dive into the clear green water. When she returned, freshened and invigorated, Crane had breakfast ready, and as soon as they had finished and seen to the mules they were off again along the floor of the Canyon.

Previously, when Tessa had stood on the Rim and imagined what it must be like at the bottom, she had seen it as a narrow place, dark within the high cliffs. And the inner canyons, the labyrinths of winding maze through dark rock, the hidden clefts that were watered by sparkling cascades, they often were like that. But much of the main Canyon was broad and open—up to eighteen miles wide, she remembered—and often the main Rim wasn't even visible. Instead, she found herself in deep valleys between mighty terraced mountain ranges, or following a wide track beside the roaring waters of the Colorado River.

And here, they began to meet other people. Hikers who had spent the night at Bright Angel or Phantom Ranch, and were now exploring the Canyon, or starting out on the long climb back to the Rim. And river-runners—groups of people on huge inflatable rafts, surging past on the white waters of the river, tumbling impossibly so that it seemed they must capsize, cheering as they survived yet another heart-stopping rapid, screaming in mock panic and shouting with delight as they emerged wet and laughing from a mass of foaming waves.

'Where do they come from? How do they get down here?' Tessa asked, as they paused to give the mules a rest and watch a particularly noisy party disappear into a steep gorge.

Crane grinned. 'They start off down here—or at least, on the river. Generally, the parties meet up in Las Vegas, then transport's laid on to the starting-point, Lees Ferry. It's a pretty interesting trip—you go through Marble Canyon, the Navajo Indian Reservation, Grand Canyon itself, Kaibab National Forest, the Hualapai Indian Reservation and Lake Mead. Takes about nine days.'

'Nine *days*!' Tessa stared at the river. 'Nine days living on a raft? That's an endurance test!'

Crane shrugged. 'Depends on what you enjoy. Some people like getting away from it all, seeing real life. That's what it is down here—real life. Away from all the nonsense that goes on up there——' he jerked his head towards the Rim '—you get to understand what it's all about. You get a different perspective. And if nine days on a raft gets people to realise that—well, it's worth it. And it's a very scenic ride. You go through all the rapids, see places like Soap Creek, Deer Creek Falls, Havasu Canyon—some of 'em places you can't see any other way. And you can have a lot of fun.' He paused as a party of hikers passed them with cheerful greetings. 'As a way to spend nine days of your life, river-running would take a lot of beating.'

They remounted the mules and continued along the track. Tessa was now growing used to the motion and beginning to feel at home with her mule. She looked around her with interest, thrilled when they caught sight of some mule deer and two coyotes, straining her eyes to see the eagles high above, following Crane's pointing finger with eagerness to pick out the hunched figure of a great blue heron standing motionless at the edge of a pool.

Tessa rode quietly along beside Crane. She felt at ease now, comfortable, in spite of the turmoil set up by their morning encounter. Perhaps it was the effect of the Canyon—perhaps its wildness, the sense that it had been here for millions of years before humanity, would still be here for millions of years afterwards, brought all one's primitive instincts to the surface. Perhaps it was no more than that. An initiation which Crane had recognised and allowed to go no further than it should.

And now the peace of the Canyon was beginning to soak into Tessa, so that she felt detached from the world she had left at the Rim, the world of cars and television, of politics and pollution and people. Crane was right, she thought, lulled by the deep silence that was—when you listened properly—no silence at all, but filled with the unceasing murmur of water, the song of birds, the rustle of soft breezes in the trees. This was the real world. It had to be.

It was about mid-afternoon, with the sun at its hottest, when they came into view of the cabin.

'That's it,' Crane said, breaking a long silence. 'That's where Grandpa lives.'

The mules halted. They had just come through a narrow gorge, a cleft through dark red rock, and rounded a corner. With an abruptness that was almost a shock, the rocks fell away on either side, leaving a broad, sunlit valley floor, green with grass and dotted with shrubs and small trees. At the far end of the valley rose a mountain, its terraces sloping towards the sky.

And in the valley, close to the stream that ran clear as glass to join the river in the main canyon, stood a long, low house—a cabin built entirely of wood and stone, looking as if it had grown from the rocks and grass among which it stood.

'Grandfather lives there?' Tessa said.

'That's right.'

Tessa sat quite still on her mule. She looked steadily at the house. It was the only building in the valley, the only sign of human habitation they had seen since coming down the steep Bright Angel Trail. Tessa saw the clutter of daily living around it, the chickens running loose, the carefully tended garden full of vegetables, the pile of logs stacked neatly for winter fires.

Was this the home of her grandfather? Was it the home of a recluse?

'Is he—is he expecting us?' She felt a return of her nervousness. It had left her during the trek down the Canyon, but if she could have abandoned the whole project at this moment, she would have done so. The thought of meeting the man hurt so badly by her mother's actions a quarter of a century earlier seemed more terrifying than ever. Suppose he refused to speak to her? Suppose he sent her away? The humiliation of having to trek back all that way without even being able to explain was too horrific to contemplate.

Would Crane have brought her all the way down here, if he'd known that his grandfather would refuse to see her? Surely not—but then she recalled Crane's hostility when they were on the Rim. Maybe he would have seen it as a just and salutary punishment. And if he'd changed since they descended into the Canyon, maybe that was just the effect of the place. It needn't make any difference to his real feelings. Was he even now anticipating her humiliation?

Tessa squared her shoulders. It wasn't up to Crane, she reminded herself. It wasn't anything to do with him. This was between her grandfather and herself, as her mother's representative. And the sooner they got the first confrontation over, the better.

'He knows we're coming,' Crane said, answering her question. 'He doesn't know exactly when. It's quite possible he's gone fishing.'

'Well,' Tessa said, urging her mule forward again, 'we'd better go and see. And if he's not there, we can wait. He'll be back some time, I suppose.'

Slowly, they rode towards the house. Long and low, it lay

basking in the warmth of the afternoon sunshine, the sparkling waters of the rushing stream reflected in the shining windows, shaded by wood-shingled eaves. In front of it there was a tiny garden, planted with the flowers of the Canyon—the desert wildflowers, the saguaro blossom which Crane had told her was the state plant of Arizona, and the scarlet flame of the Indian paintbrush—shaded by the spreading spines of a giant ocotillo. At the side, there was an outbuilding which Tessa guessed was probably a stable, and at the back there was a veranda below which the chickens she'd seen were gathering to peck up freshly thrown corn.

So her grandfather must be somewhere nearby. Tessa felt her heart jerk and her breath came suddenly faster.

Crane rode up to the veranda, dismounted from his mule and threw the reins over the rail.

'Grandpa!' He leapt up the steps and disappeared into the dim interior. 'Grandpa—it's me. Got a visitor for you.'

Tessa got down slowly from her mule. Uncertainly, she waited. The sun was hot on her head and it was very quiet. The chickens had retreated and were eyeing her from under a nearby bush. She heard a sound from the door leading on to the veranda and turned quickly.

For a moment, she thought it must be Crane standing there. And then the man moved forward, into the sunlight, and she knew that this must be her grandfather.

Tessa gazed at him, her emotions confused. This was no decrepit old man. Todd Mellor, at over seventy, was still an imposing figure. And it was difficult, at first sight, to decide just which was his most striking feature.

There was his thick, plentiful hair, white now where once it must have been black, the eyebrows that had grown greyer and shaggier with the years, and the skin, leathery, deeply creased with the seams of sunlight and age.

And the eyes—dark and fathomless, glowering like those of a captive eagle, piercing as needles. The lines of the face, lean and hawk-like, with a profile that was almost harsh, a mouth that would never compromise. The lean, sparse height that only muscle could save from being gaunt, sinewy rather than rippling, but still, she guessed, containing both strength and power.

And last of all, as he came slowly down the steps, she saw the lithe, animal grace, even in this man who must be almost seventy-five years old.

Her grandfather came to the bottom of the steps and there was a long silence. Tessa stood quite still under his scrutiny. This was quite a moment for him too, she reminded herself. He was meeting his granddaughter for the first time. A granddaughter he'd probably never expected to see, the daughter of his child who had left him when scarcely older than Tessa was now. It must need some taking in.

'So you're Betsy's girl.'

His voice was strong, resonant. Tessa looked at him, quailing a little under that piercing stare, but standing her ground. She didn't know what sort of reception he intended to give her—maybe he was going to tell her to turn round and go right back home. But she had a feeling that she had quite a lot in common with this old man, and that they probably both shared a stubborn streak.

She was Betsy's daughter. Nothing of what had happened had been her fault, and she didn't believe there had ever been any need for bitterness. And she was quite prepared to tell him so.

'Yes, I'm Tessa. I'm your granddaughter.'

There was a touch of defiance in her tone, as if she were daring him to deny it. But Todd Mellor only grunted, his expression inscrutable. He came a little closer, still examining her.

'You're mighty like Betsy when she was a girl.'

'Yes, I know—people say we're very much alike.'

'People in England, that'd be.'

'We haven't been anywhere else,' Tessa said coolly.

Todd grunted again. There was no way of telling whether he was pleased with her or not.

'You've come a mighty long way to see me. Why'd you do that?' he asked.

'Why shouldn't I?' Tessa countered, her heart sinking. He wasn't going to give an inch, not an inch! He was as obstinate as ever, she thought, and there was surely as little chance of winning him over.

'After nearly twenty-five years, I wonder you hadn't forgotten all about me.' He was watching her closely, and Tessa realised he was testing her, throwing out provocative remarks just to see how she would react. Just like Crane!

'We would have liked to come before,' she said, still keeping her tone cool. 'It just wasn't possible. And my mother isn't well enough to travel anywhere now. She sent me to—to——' The sudden memory of just how ill her mother was brought an ache of tears into her throat, and she choked a little and turned away. She knew that her mother hadn't told Todd the full facts of her illness, and it wasn't his fault that he didn't know ... but even if he did know, would his attitude be any less intransigent? It isn't going to be any use, she thought despairingly—it's been a complete waste of time and money, coming all this way. I would have been better off staying at home with Mum, looking after her—enjoying what little time we'd got left ...

Her grandfather didn't move. When she turned back, he was still watching her. His face didn't seem to have changed, but as they looked at each other he said with a very slight softening in his tone, 'You'd better come along inside. Dare say it's hot out here for you. Crane's making us a cool drink—you'll feel better after that.'

He turned and went up the veranda steps, leaving Tessa to follow. Bleakly, she did so. She was convinced now that her journey had been wasted, that there was no way of getting through to this stubborn old man. No way of getting him to understand the pain his years of silence had brought to his daughter, no way of bringing them together again.

If only she'd managed to make Crane see it, he might have helped. But instead he'd painted a picture of grief that had aroused all her own sympathy. And she knew that they would never understand how life had been back in England, how quickly the years had flown, how there had never been time—never an opportunity . . .

How many families drifted apart in this way? she wondered. Parted first by a misunderstanding, meaning to get back in touch, meaning to visit and never quite managing it. Until, one day, it was too late.

Inside, the house was cool and spacious, with a long living-room that took up most of the length. The furniture was of heavy, polished wood, rough-hewn as if carved straight from the trunks and limbs of great trees and softened with cushions of furs and skins. The wooden floor, scattered with thick sheepskin rugs, glowed with rich colour, and the windows were hung with curtains of muted reds, oranges and browns. In the middle of the room was a long table with a huge bowl of flowers and leaves on it.

Crane was making drinks at a bench in the corner. He turned as they came in and handed Tessa a tall, cool glass. She drank gratefully.

'Well, here she is, Grandpa,' Crane said after a few

minutes' silence. 'What do you think of her?'

Todd Mellor set down his glass. He looked at Tessa, then at Crane. She wondered if his expression ever altered—perhaps it was fixed in those dour lines, had been for years. Perhaps that was what losing almost your entire family did to you.

I ought to make allowances, she thought. It was bad enough for Mum—but wasn't it worse for him? Losing her, losing Joe and Willa—all within little more than a year. Is it surprising he's bitter?

'She's mighty like Betsy, to look at,' Todd repeated at last.

'I thought that,' Crane agreed. 'From what I remembered.'

'And you'd remember Betsy at about the same age.' Todd looked at Tessa again. 'Same hair—shorter, like they have it these days, but the same—same eyes, same stubborn little chin and mouth. Got that from Mary, she did—that's your grandmother,' he added to Tessa. 'She was a fine woman—came out here to work at El Tovar and as soon as I set eyes on her, I knew she was the woman for me. But she wouldn't say yes until her year was out.' He shook his head, eyes misting. 'Yes, she could be stubborn too—I guess when we got wed and started a family we kind of multiplied it. But we had a good marriage—just didn't last long enough.'

Tessa said nothing. Betsy had told her how her mother had died when she was only sixteen years old. Perhaps that was why Todd had been so possessive, so against her leaving the Canyon.

'You a handful, like your mother was?' he shot at her suddenly, and Crane laughed.

'No, I'm not,' Tessa said indignantly. 'And if Mum was——'

'Yes? If she was?' It was a challenge, and Tessa couldn't

help rising to it. She forgot her resolution about making allowances—did this intractable old man *need* allowances made for him? She lifted her chin and met his eyes squarely.

'If she was, maybe it wasn't entirely her fault. Maybe you made her that way—did that ever occur to you?' Head up, eyes sparkling, she gave him look for look. 'You weren't an easy man to have as a father, if all my mother says is true— and I don't see any reason at all to disbelieve her. All right, so you'd lost your wife and that didn't make it easy for you—but it wasn't any better for her, losing her mother. And instead of realising that, giving her a bit of comfort and understanding, what did you do? You kept her on a tight rein, gave her hardly any freedom, wanted to know everything she did, everyone she met. If you want my opinion, it's no wonder she ran away! It was the only way she could ever get free of you.' She stopped, biting her lip, regretting those last words. She hadn't come here to hurt and quarrel with her grandfather. Now he would turn her out, tell her to go, and there would never be any chance of a reconciliation. 'I'm sorry,' she said quickly. 'I didn't mean to say that—not at once—I mean——'

To her surprise, Todd's face relaxed, the stern creases crinkling with sudden ironic humour. 'You mean you were going to save it for later?'

'No, I don't—I mean—oh——' She turned to Crane and saw that he was laughing openly at her confusion. 'And *you're* no help!'

'Any reason why I should be?' he countered, and she shook her head and turned away.

'No. No reason at all.' Swinging back, she faced them both. 'All right, it was a mistake, coming here. There was never any use in it, was there? But I had to try—for my mother's sake, I had to try.' She paused, looking down at the polished wood of the long table. 'I'll go,' she said in a low voice. 'I'll go as soon as you can take me, Crane. And I'll tell my mother what she wanted to know.' She raised her eyes to her grandfather's face. 'That you're well and strong and—I suppose—happy. And I'll tell her about Joe and Willa, too—if she's strong enough. It may be over twenty years too late, but I know she'll want to mourn them. She'll spend the last part of her life grieving for them, when it should have been over long ago.' Tessa's face was pale and set, her eyes dangerously bright. She could feel the tears in them and lifted her head so that they wouldn't spill over. 'And from now on, you can forget all about us. We won't write again. I can see now that it's never been any good.' She turned away again, making blindly for the door.

A strong, muscular hand gripped her arm, jerking her back. She found herself thrust into a big armchair and held there. Panting, breathless with astonishment, she stared up into the dark, stormy face that confronted her.

'Now listen here,' Crane said, his voice threaded with anger. 'Just you listen to me for a minute. You talk as if it all depended on you and what you want—this visit. Well, maybe you did come here of your own accord—but you're not the only one involved in it now, not by a long chalk. You've got me in it too, and Grandpa. And you don't walk out on it now, just because the going's tough. Just how easy did you expect it to be, anyway? Were we all supposed to shout with joy just because you chose to come out here and upset all our lives, reminding us of things that happened a long time ago?' He took his hands away and stood up, while Tessa rubbed her arms. 'You've stirred things up, coming out here, and you're staying to face it out. Give it a go. If it still won't work—OK, you can go back to your little town in Sussex, England, and we'll *all* forget each other—if we can. But you can't come here and stir up a hornet's nest, and then walk away and leave other people to settle it down same as it was before. D'you get that?'

Tessa blinked. Half of what he said made sense—but whose side was he on? It sounded almost as if he *wanted* her to stay, wanted her to succeed with the reconciliation; but he'd never given any hint that way before. His bitter hostility, followed by curt indifference, had given her quite the opposite impression. But she had to admit that he was right in saying that by coming here she had stirred up old passions, old pains, and that now she'd done that she ought to stay and see the consequences through. She couldn't just go off and leave the situation.

All forget each other—if we can, Crane had said. Staring up at him, still fingering the tender spots where his fingers had gripped her arms, seeing the tiger that lurked behind those agate eyes ready to pounce if she should so much as move, Tessa knew that whatever happened in this secret valley, she would never be able to forget them. Crane and Todd were members of her family. And although they had been until now mere shadows, no more than names, they had become real, vibrant personalities. She could never forget them now.

Especially Crane.

'D'you get that?' he repeated harshly. 'Do you understand?' And he gripped her arms again and gave her a small shake.

'All right!' she snapped at him, restored by the movement. 'All right, I understand—you think I ought to stay—get to know Grandfather, I suppose. You think *he* ought to have the chance to get to know *me*.' She looked past the lean, strong body to where her grandfather was watching them with hooded eyes. 'And suppose he doesn't want to know me? Suppose he'd rather I went?'

'Then he'll say so,' Crane said equably, and straightened

up again. 'What d'you say, Grandpa? Does Tessa stay—or does she give it all up and go back? It's up to you—what do *you* want?'

They looked across at him, Tessa feeling a sudden, unexpected anxiety. Crane's words had gone home to her. She knew that she couldn't go back a failure, without having even tried. She ought to make a real effort to make friends with her grandfather. And it ought to be possible—after all, her mother *had* loved him, strict though he'd been. She *had* suffered through being cut off from him.

Tessa had come here for her mother's sake. For her mother's sake, she must stay.

She stood up and walked across the room to the old man. He was like a wood carving himself, she thought, brown and hard and still in this big room. She touched his arm and raised her eyes to his face.

'What do you say, Grandfather?' she asked quietly, hardly realising that this was the first time she had addressed him by this name. 'Do you want me to stay—for a little while? So that we can get to know each other?'

And, to her surprise, she saw a sudden shine in the old, dark eyes. The mouth that had seemed so uncompromising twisted a little, and the creased face relaxed slightly.

He spoke gruffly, as if denying the possibility of giving way, and his words were not exactly fulsome. But for Tessa, believing that she had seen a glimpse of the man behind that iron façade, they were enough.

'Seems all the same to me,' he said, turning away, perhaps so that she shouldn't see the expression on his face. 'Stay if you like. I dare say you'll be glad to go back, soon enough.'

He went across the room to the kitchen bench where Crane had made the drinks, and stood fiddling with the bottles there. He kept his back to them for a full minute, then turned abruptly.

'Well? What are you doing, just standing there, the pair of you? There's two mules out there want rubbing down and watering. Hadn't you better get out and see to 'em? Or are you waiting for a couple of servants to appear? Because if you are, you've got a good long wait ahead of you.'

Crane chuckled and disappeared through the door. Tessa waited a moment longer, hoping for a smile or even a glance from her grandfather before she followed him. But Todd had turned away and didn't look at her again.

Clearly, he had compromised as far as he was able to, at the moment. The task ahead of her wasn't going to be easy. But she had made a start. And as she went out into the sunshine she felt oddly optimistic.

If only she could be sure of breaking down Crane's hostility too.

CHAPTER FIVE

LIFE on the floor of the Grand Canyon was, Tessa soon discovered, a very different affair from on the Rim—topside, her grandfather called it. Basically—and it was certainly back to basics down here, where your grocery order was flown in once a month and fresh food had to be either caught or grown—it was a backwoods life, yet with visitors passing through like beings from another world. Tessa never quite got used to the idea that the hikers who passed their door had been up there in the real world only days, even hours, earlier, and could return to it just as quickly.

Already she could understand her grandfather's love for the Canyon. But that didn't mean he was easy to know. And she still wasn't at all sure that he wanted her to know him; his leathery face wore a closed look that told her she was there only on sufferance.

'You'd better sleep in there,' he told her that first evening, jerking his head towards one of the two bedrooms that led off the main room of the cabin. 'It's smaller'n the other one, but Crane'll need to bunk in with me. Unless you want to sleep out?' he added as Crane came through the door with a bucket of water from the spring.

'Don't mind. It's pleasant weather—cooler outside, I guess.' Crane set the bucket down and turned his attention to the salad vegetables that Todd had just brought in from his garden. 'Anyway, I won't be here after tonight—got to get back.'

Tessa stared at him with a consternation that surprised her. Crane leaving? Leaving her down here, alone with the grandfather who so far hadn't shown her any welcome? Or did he intend that she should go back with him—in which case she wouldn't have had a chance to make things up?

But why should Crane's presence make any difference, anyway? His own attitude was equally hostile—at least, where her mother was concerned. Feeling a blush creep into her cheeks at the memory of yesterday in the pool and this morning as they lay close in their sleeping-bags, Tessa was glad of the dimness of the room. Maybe it was better after all if Crane weren't here. His presence was a complication, his attitude to her ambivalent and disturbing.

'I suppose you have to get back for the air trips,' she said, making up her mind not to let him see that his departure mattered to her—not even sure that it did.

'That's right. Can't take too much time off at this time of year, when we're just starting to get busy. Not fair on Emery, or the others.' Crane finished washing the salad and began to set it out on plates. 'All right to eat this ham, Grandpa?'

'Sure. It needs to be eaten soon.' The old man turned to Tessa. 'I only get groceries every four weeks—after that I'm on my own. But there's plenty of good food down here—I keep hens and there's some good meals swimming past in the creek. Grow my own vegetables—bake my own bread. I don't want for much.'

'No, I can see that.' The cabin was comfortable with a practical homeliness that appealed to Tessa. There was no

The more
you love romance . . .
the more
you'll love this offer

FREE!

Mail this heart today! (see inside)

Join us on a Harlequin Honeymoon
and we'll give you
4 free books
A free makeup mirror and brush kit
And a free mystery gift

IT'S A HARLEQUIN HONEYMOON— A SWEETHEART OF A FREE OFFER!
HERE'S WHAT YOU GET:

1. **Four New Harlequin Romance® Novels—FREE!**
   Take a Harlequin Honeymoon with your four exciting romances—yours FREE from Harlequin Reader Service. Each of these hot-off-the-press novels brings you the passion and tenderness of today's greatest love stories...your free passports to bright new worlds of love and foreign adventure.

2. **A Lighted Makeup Mirror and Brush Kit—FREE!**

   This lighted makeup mirror and brush kit allows plenty of light for those quick touch-ups. It operates on two easy-to-replace batteries and bulbs (batteries not included). It holds everything you need for a perfect finished look yet is small enough to slip into your purse or pocket— 4-⅛" x 3" closed.

3. **An Exciting Mystery Bonus—FREE!**
   You'll be thrilled with this surprise gift. It will be the source of many compliments, as well as a useful and attractive addition to your home.

4. **Money-Saving Home Delivery!**
   Join Harlequin Reader Service and enjoy the convenience of previewing eight new books every month delivered right to your home. Each book is yours for only $1.99—26¢ less per book than what you pay in stores. And there is no extra charge for postage and handling. Great savings plus total convenience add up to a sweetheart of a deal for you!

5. **Free Newsletter**
   It's *heart to heart*, the indispensable insider's look at our most popular writers, upcoming books, even recipes from your favorite authors.

6. **More Surprise Gifts**
   Because our home subscribers are our most valued readers, we'll be sending you additional free gifts from time to time—as a token of our appreciation.

START YOUR HARLEQUIN HONEYMOON TODAY—JUST COMPLETE, DETACH AND MAIL YOUR FREE-OFFER CARD

Get your fabulous gifts
ABSOLUTELY FREE!

MAIL THIS CARD TODAY.

START YOUR
HARLEQUIN HONEYMOON TODAY.
JUST COMPLETE, DETACH AND MAIL YOUR
FREE OFFER CARD.

If offer card below is missing, write to: Harlequin Reader Service, 901 Fuhrmann Blvd.
P.O. Box 1394, Buffalo, NY, 14240-1394

DETACH AND MAIL TODAY!

BUSINESS REPLY CARD

First Class Permit No. 717 Buffalo, NY

Postage will be paid by addressee

Harlequin Reader Service ®
901 Fuhrmann Blvd.
P.O. Box 1394
Buffalo, NY 14240-9963

NO POSTAGE
NECESSARY
IF MAILED
IN THE
UNITED STATES

television to dominate the room with its blank grey eye, no electric fire to throw out a soulless heat. But the walls were lined with full bookshelves, a tape recorder lay on a table with a scatter of cassettes around it, and the big fireplace was already laid with logs for when the nights grew chilly.

At the kitchen end of the room there was a large refrigerator—run by Todd's own generator, she had learned—and a small electric cooker. But there was also a large woodstove on which he did most of his winter cooking, and Tessa could imagine that the stove and the open fire between them would keep the whole house warm.

'What are winters like here?' she asked, as Crane set the plates out on the big table. 'Do you stay here right through?'

Todd shook his head. 'I generally go topside for a couple of months when the weather's at its worst. Stay with Crane. But only because the phone might be unreliable then, and planes might have a job to get supplies down to me. Winter's a good time down here, if you don't object to your own company.'

'You don't get many visitors then?'

Todd laughed shortly, sounding very like Crane.

'Visitors? Hikers, you mean? No—not a lot. Not many hikers like the idea of getting down here through deep snow, with the trails all iced-up. That's the beauty of it, see. Real peace and quiet. No chance of people rolling up out of nowhere and expecting you to provide them with food and drinks because they didn't take the trouble to find out there's no smart restaurants down here. You can be absolutely sure of being left alone.' He ate quickly, biting at his food as if it were an enemy. 'Just you and the snow, and the animals. That's the Canyon at its best.'

Tessa watched him apprehensively. She could sense the tension in him, the anger that she supposed must still be directed at her mother. But there was nothing she could say—not now, anyway. The subject would have to be raised, she and her grandfather would have to have it out—but not yet. They both needed time, time to accustom themselves to each other, time to circle round like wary dogs before facing the issue that lay between them like a disputed bone.

Later that evening, she and Crane went for a walk along the creek, leaving Todd to listen to some music on his tape recorder. Dusk had fallen and the night's darkness was gathering in corners, ready to spread itself like a blanket over the grassy bed of the Canyon. Owls called, their cries floating back and forth, multiplied by echoes from the towering rock walls.

'Trouble with coming down here,' Crane said, breaking their silence, 'is that I never want to go back topside.'

'Would you like to live here all the time?' Tessa looked up at the stars that were prickling the sky above. 'I can see why Grandfather does. Everything seems so far away—so unimportant.'

'Not all the time, no. Not unless I had some purpose in living down here.' He looked down at her. 'You mean he's running away?'

Tessa paused. Had she meant that? 'I don't think so,' she said doubtfully. 'But I suppose it could be that. I don't blame him—he's had a hard time, losing his family as he did. Down here, where it's a world of its own, away from everything that we think is real—well, he can forget it, a little anyway. Perhaps that's the only way he can cope.'

'You do admit he's had it tough, then?'

Tessa immediately reacted to the grim note in Crane's voice. She controlled herself and answered steadily, 'Yes, of course I do. I don't admit it was my mother's fault. And I still feel she ought to have been told what happened to your parents. Joe was her brother. She should have been given the chance to grieve, the chance to *do* something.'

Tessa stopped, leaning against a rock. The peace of the night had faded and she felt anger churning inside her. How had they got on to this subject again? It seemed that whenever she and Crane began to find some rapport, their family history intruded and spoiled it. A sudden pang struck at her heart. How, she wondered bleakly, would things have been between us if we hadn't been linked—and divided—in this way?

But then—they would never have met . . .

'She might not have been able to come back then, she was expecting me,' she said quietly, 'But she would have *known*. Perhaps she could have come later—the next year, the year after. She could have written—phoned. She *did* write—you know that, she wrote all through the years. But if she'd known—her letters would have been different.'

Crane grunted and walked on, leaving Tessa to follow or not as she chose. After some hesitation, she walked after him. Tomorrow, he would be gone, back to the Rim; and in spite of their differences, she didn't want him to go still angry with her—and with her mother. If she could win him over, show him that the bitterness he and his grandfather had shared was wrong—she might have a chance with Todd.

And, without any idea why, she realised that Crane's own opinion was becoming important to her.

'Please,' she said, catching up with him, 'don't let's

quarrel. It's crazy; none of this had anything to do with us—it isn't our fight. Can't we be friends?' She looked up at him, searching the darkness that shadowed his face. 'I thought this morning that you wanted that too,' she said simply, quite unprepared for the effect of her words.

Crane took a step towards her. The tension emanating from his body caught at her like a net, paralysing her. Rigid, she stood perfectly still as his hand touched her arm, gripped it with a cruel ferocity. He was close to her now, so close that she could feel the warmth of his body, the tiny breeze of his breath on her cheek. It came quickly, matching the rise and fall of his chest, so near that it brushed her own taut breasts. She wanted to move away— *had* to move away—but even as she made the effort, his grip on her arm tightened and his other arm came round her shoulders to hold her firmly against him.

'Friends?' he muttered, his voice thick in his throat. 'Friends? Is that really what you want, Tessa—friendship between you and me? Do you really believe that's possible?'

Tessa was shaking in his arms, her body trembling so violently that if he had not been holding her she would have fallen. Her heart was going wild inside her, thumping and kicking like a trapped animal beating its way to freedom. Her breathing was so fast that it seemed impossible that she was actually taking in any air at all, and deep within her she could feel something twisting, twining, tingling—a sweet, intolerable pain from which there was no relief.

Crane brought his head down to hers, blotting out the clouds and stars, and as his lips touched her mouth Tessa's eyes closed. Weakness invaded her; her limbs were suddenly heavy and she could barely manage to raise her arms to cling to him as her head fell back and her lips parted. A soft whimper sounded in her throat, answered by a deep groan from his, and when her eyelids fluttered open for a moment she could see the stars wheeling above as if set in motion by the urgency of their coming together.

Crane moved one hand down her body, caressing her waist, her buttocks, her slender thigh. With a sigh, she shifted and settled herself closer against him. Her strength was returning, but she no longer wanted to escape; instead, she responded to his demands with an urgency of her own, seeking his lips with hers, letting her tongue play with his, flicking it against his mouth and teeth as his thrust against hers. As his hand slid up her body again, she stretched and twisted so that it could cup her breast, and when he touched her hardened nipple, she gasped and moved against him with a sensuousness she hadn't known herself capable of.

'Tessa!' he muttered against her hair. 'Oh, my God, Tessa . . . don't do that . . . for God's sake, don't do it . . .!'

'Don't do what?' She was drunk with emotion, intoxicated by the beauty of the Canyon, the sense of being in another world, high on the surge of desire that had taken them both by surprise. 'Don't kiss you? Don't let you kiss me? You started it, Crane.' She wound her arms around his neck, yearning for the contact again, hungry for his lips. But he pulled himself gently away, holding her at arm's length now, and she stared at him, feeling suddenly cold and bereft.

'I know I started it, Tessa,' he said quietly. 'It's my fault—I'm not trying to deny that. But if you knew what— oh hell! I'd better not say. It's maybe better that you don't know.'

He turned abruptly away, leaving Tessa standing alone,

feeling suddenly vulnerable.

'Know what?' she asked, her voice trembling. 'Crane, what is it? What's happening?'

'Nothing's happening.' His voice was harsh now, and she flinched. 'Nothing's happening, nothing at all. It's just this place—this place, together with a man and a woman. It isn't you, Tessa—it isn't even me. It's just what being down here does to people, and it means nothing.' He whipped round as violently as he'd turned away from her. 'You understand that? *Nothing*. You've got to forget it—pretend it never happened.' He was gripping her arms again, shaking her. If nothing had happened, Tessa thought confusedly, it had certainly had a very odd effect on him.

'All right,' she said, her voice throbbing with reaction. 'All right! You don't have to shake me to pieces. So nothing happened! Well, that's fine with me. I've every intention of forgetting it—every intention of pretending we were never here. And the sooner it's true and you're back on the Rim where I can't see you and don't have to listen to you, the better!'

She'd been right, she thought angrily, rubbing her arms as he let her go. He was nothing but a womaniser, an opportunist who had to make the most of every chance. So far he had been recalled to sanity just in time—but each time, he had gone a little further and she quailed at the thought of what might happen if they were thrown together much more.

And the worst part of it was her own reaction. Why was it? Why could she apparently not resist him, why did she have so little defence?

Perhaps, she thought miserably as she followed him back along the trail, they shared more than the link of family history. Perhaps they shared something darker, a side of their own natures that recognised its own kind.

Whatever the reason—it was definitely a good job that Crane was going back tomorrow. For with him around, Tessa was never going to know any peace of mind.

Left alone at last with her grandfather, Tessa felt at something of a loss.

Until Crane went, it wasn't so bad. There was plenty to do: having breakfast all together—hash browns and ham, made by Todd, with plenty of coffee—feeding the hens while Todd and Crane went off to look at the creek, washing-up, and packing food and water for Crane to take with him. Listening to the two men talking, Tessa felt comfortably invisible. Not that feeling invisible was a sensation she normally liked much—but in this situation, it was welcome, giving her a breathing-space in which to find her bearings.

Last night was still fresh in her memory—all too fresh, she thought ruefully, considering she had told Crane it was as good as forgotten. But she had found it dismayingly hard to forget, impossible to put out of her mind. Over and over again, as she lay in the narrow bed trying to sleep, she had woken convinced that she could still feel Crane's arms around her, turning in his imagined embrace to seek his lips with her own. Over and over again, she had returned to consciousness with a sense of loss, quickly followed by a guilty anger that she could be so weak, so easily seduced.

And it didn't help that she was all too well aware that Crane was close, somewhere outside on the mattress he'd dragged out from the house. Her body in a turmoil of longing, Tessa had held herself rigid, refusing even to acknowledge her need to go out to him, to lie down close to his body, feel his arms around her once more, his lips on hers . . .

It was crazy! They weren't in love—they didn't even *like* each other! This attraction, whatever it was—it was totally unexpected in both of them. Tessa wished that she had never come to the Grand Canyon, never discovered this aspect of herself. It would never have surfaced at home, in Sussex, she was sure. Never have been suspected if she had been content to stay there, settle down and be an ordinary wife and mother.

But she knew now that the life she had seemed destined for in England was no longer possible for her. Perhaps it never had been; perhaps, because of her ancestry, she had always been doomed to leave the leafy byways of Sussex and come back to the wild grandeur of her mother's home.

Perhaps there was something here she had to do, besides mend the rift between Todd Mellor and his daughter.

Something to do with Crane . . .?

Tessa shivered. The bed seemed suddenly hard, too hard for sleeping. She looked out of the window and saw the soaring cliffs, the stars high above.

The mystic power of the Grand Canyon seemed very close—and very oppressive.

'Well, that's it,' Todd remarked as they stood together watching Crane jog slowly away down the trail on his mule. 'Shan't be seeing him again for a while.'

He turned away and went back towards the house, with Tessa following him uncertainly. Now that they were alone, she wasn't quite sure what to do. Not that it mattered a lot, she supposed—they had all the time necessary now.

There was no escape from each other, down here. And in spite of her long journey to get here, there didn't seem to be any particular hurry to introduce the subject of her mother and the quarrel. It was better to let it arise naturally, when Todd felt ready for it.

It was an odd, quiet sort of day. Tessa, determined not to hurry her grandfather and reminding herself that he was, after all, an old man and might well need time to adjust to the idea of having a granddaughter around, tried to remain as unobtrusive as possible. She tidied her small bedroom but didn't interfere with the rest of the house; watched as Todd tended the animals, holding the sack of corn when he fed the hens, and taking care to groom and fuss over the mule Crane had left behind for her use. When Todd fetched gardening tools and made for the vegetable patch, she asked if she could do some weeding, and paid close attention while he pointed out to her which plants she should pull out. But in such a well kept garden, her job was soon over and she went into the house to prepare some lunch from the salad vegetables in the refrigerator and the ham left from last night's meal.

Todd came in, saw her preparations and grunted. He washed and sat down at the table.

'You'll be finding it a mite different here from England,' he said after a while.

'It depends what you mean by different.' Tessa sliced a tomato. 'The scenery's different, of course—we don't have much in the way of rock, and certainly no canyons or mountains, not in Sussex, anyway. But other things are the same—the important things.'

'Important things?'

'People,' she said steadily. 'The way they behave. The

way they live. There's not so much difference in those
things anywhere.'

Todd grunted again. 'You think so?'

'Yes, I do. People are people, wherever they are. Where
you live doesn't alter that.'

'Hm,' he said. 'I'm not so sure. Places can make a deal of
difference, in my experience. Maybe you haven't been
about enough to realise that yet. Stay down here long, and
you will.' He shot her a sharp glance from under his shaggy
brows. 'Don't you feel it already? The difference in
yourself, being down here?'

Tessa hesitated. Hadn't she thought, only last night, of
the effect the Grand Canyon was having on her? Hadn't
she been aware of its power ever since she'd first seen it from
the air, a great slash in the face of the earth?

But that wasn't really the place, she argued. It was
something in herself, called out by the environment—not
caused by it. A mere arrangement of rocks and water and
sky couldn't make you do things that weren't already in
your nature. Not even if the arrangement was one of the
seven wonders of the world.

'How long have you lived down here, Grandfather?' she
asked, avoiding his own question.

'How long?' The leathery face creased in thought. 'A few
years. Ten—twelve—I haven't counted lately. Since Crane
grew up, anyway, and took on responsibility for himself.'
He took another slice of ham. 'He's been a grand kid to me,
Crane. Don't really know what I'd have done without him
around.'

Tessa was silent. Had there been an implied rebuke in
her grandfather's voice, or was he merely stating a fact? No

doubt Crane *had* been a good grandson, even though there was no blood tie. And so he should have been—for Todd had taken him in when Joe and Willa had died, had brought him up, been grandparent and both parents to him. And he had done it in the midst of his own grief—while her mother had been in England, enjoying a marriage that was happy in spite of its difficulties, with no idea of the havoc that was being wreaked in her family back home.

But that wasn't her fault! Tessa argued hotly, inside her head—and for the first time was shocked to find a second voice joining in. A tiny voice that was nevertheless disconcertingly clear, a voice that asked: But could she have done more? Could she have found out some other way? Was writing letters quite enough?

Hastily she got to her feet, cleared away the plates and brought a bowl of fruit to the table. It must have been among the grocery order flown in, she thought, or did Todd somehow grow his own down here? The soil seemed fertile, all the vegetables strong and healthy. She wondered if Todd baked cakes for himself as well as bread, and whether he might like her to make some.

The old man was watching her quizzically.

'You don't have to wait on me, you know. I know how to look after myself—don't need a woman's touch about the place.'

Tessa flushed. 'I know—I can see you don't. But I have to do something—I don't want to be waited on either.'

He nodded. 'Fair enough.' He took an apple and bit into it with teeth that were still strong. 'Get on well with Crane, do you?'

The question took Tessa by surprise. She opened her

mouth to say 'No' but the word didn't come. And it wasn't really true any more, she discovered. From her dislike of him when they had first met, she seemed to have progressed through a variety of emotions. She'd been angry with him—exasperated by him—she'd fought and argued and disagreed with him. But there had also, she remembered, been moments when she'd felt in accord with him, an accord more perfect and close than she'd ever experienced before. There had been moments when she'd felt deeply content to be where he was; moments that were all too short, yet held a promise she dared not examine.

And there had been other moments too—those moments she'd tried, and failed, to forget, when her body had clamoured for his and her desire had wiped everything else from her reeling mind. When she had needed him as she had never needed anyone or anything before. Moments of deep and agonising frustration when Crane himself had denied her what she yearned for.

But she could hardly tell her grandfather all that.

'I don't really know him well yet,' she said cautiously, keeping her face turned away.

'Not know him! After two days on the trail?' Todd snorted. 'Well, he's not an easy man to know, I'll grant you that. He doesn't give much away. But I can tell you this——' he leaned forward, holding up one hand with its fingers extended '—you won't find a finer man than Crane Mellor if you travel the world looking. No—that you won't. He could have gone anywhere, done anything, Crane could. But he didn't; he chose to stay here, where he'd grown up, and make a success of his life in his own home. And that's just what he's done.'

'Is it?' Tessa chose her own apple, not looking at him.

'Is it?' Todd stared at her. 'What do you mean, is it? I'm *telling* you. There's no question.'

'No?' Tessa looked up at last, meeting her grandfather's gaze with eyes that were as dark as his own. She hadn't meant to start any arguments as early as this, but perhaps there was no avoiding them. Neither of them could pretend that this was an ordinary family visit—too much lay between them. 'I'm not so sure. Has Crane really made a success of his life? Oh, he runs a successful airline, taking people for trips round the Canyon, I know that. I'm not suggesting that isn't a success, or that he ought to be head of Pan-Am instead. But that isn't all there is to life, is it?' She saw a frown gathering on the deeply lined face. 'There are other things that are important. People. Relationships.' She took a deep breath. 'Love.'

Now for it, she thought, watching for storm signals. Now for the fury to break out—the fury he's been saving up all these years for my mother.

But when Todd spoke, his voice was surprisingly mild.

'And that's what you think is important for a successful life?' he said thoughtfully.

'Yes, it is. And Crane doesn't seem to have been at all successful, as far as love goes.' Tessa gave him a steady look. 'Maybe you know why.'

She waited for a terse response, a sign that this time she had gone too far. But Todd said nothing, just gazed at her with those dark, hooded eyes as if he were genuinely considering what she had said. Then he nodded his head. It was as if nothing she had said had surprised him in any way—as if he'd expected it. And his next words told her why.

'I thought as much.' He got up from his chair and went

over to the corner of the room, where several fishing-rods stood leaning together. 'You look just like your mother did when she went away. You sound like her too.' He chose a rod and turned to look at her, and once again his face was like a piece of wood, expressionless, immovable. 'There's no arguing with a young woman once she gets those kinds of ideas into her head. I'm going down to the creek to see what I can catch. I'll see you at supper-time.'

It was a clear instruction to her to keep out of his way for the rest of the afternoon. He went out, leaving Tessa sitting at the table with her apple still in her hand. Slowly, she laid it down and looked helplessly at the open door.

He wasn't even going to discuss it; he wasn't even going to listen. He was just going to put up with her for as long as she chose to stay, and he didn't intend to let her any further into his mind or his heart than she had already reached—which was nowhere. Her mission was hopeless—and always had been.

The only person who was going to be affected by it in any way was herself. And when she thought of returning to England, leaving all this behind and going back to the soft countryside of Sussex, her heart sank.

What had it done to her, coming to this strange, wild place? And how was she ever going to be able to settle down again as before?

CHAPTER SIX

SOMEWHERE up in the blue sky above the Grand Canyon, there was an aeroplane. Tessa could hear its low, steady drone, like the murmur of bees among the tall, swaying grasses. She shaded her eyes, staring up, but couldn't see it.

Was it Crane, somewhere up there, taking his tourists for a dramatic flight between the cliffs and *mesas* of the 'boss ditch of the world'? Was he even now plunging them into the jaws of some terrifying abyss, listening with amusement to their shrieks and gasps, proud of the reaction his home territory could produce in people who lived in less spectacular places? Wild, beautiful, savage, uncompromising—the Grand Canyon was all of these, and couldn't fail to affect those who came here. No wonder so many of those qualities had seeped into the men who had spent their lives among its clefts and gullies—men like Crane, and her grandfather, Todd.

The plane was in sight now, a red fleck against the blue of the sky. There was no way of telling whether Crane were flying it, or even whether it might be one of his fleet. With a sigh, Tessa turned back to her weeding. It occurred to her that she spent far too much time staring at the sky, looking for planes.

After several days in the Canyon, Tessa and her grandfather had evolved a kind of routine. Without ever discussing the matter, they had come to an amicable agreement over how their days should be spent, Tessa fitting in as far as possible with Todd's ways, while he too had presumably made some changes. Presumably, she qualified, because she had no idea how he really lived while alone—although from the amount of books and music cassettes lying about, she guessed that he spent a good deal of time reading and listening.

Tessa had been dismayed when he first picked up a book and began to read, guessing that he was deliberately shutting himself away from her. But the music was something they could both share. It brought them closer—whether Todd wanted it to or not. And it was during the next evening, when darkness had fallen and the Canyon was once more wrapped in its night-blue gown of mystery, that he began to talk to her, telling her stories of the old days.

'The Canyon's been known to white men since the sixteenth century,' he told her as they sat out on the veranda after supper, the faint strains of Sibelius sounding from the room behind them. 'Spaniards, they were, the men who first came here. Didn't think too much of it, by all accounts. It wasn't for another three hundred years—in 1869—that Powell led the first expedition through by boat.' He filled his pipe and gave her his sharp glance. 'There were Indians here, though ... Navajo—Havasupai—Hopi. They knew the Canyon well. It was home to them.'

And your mother was one of them, Tessa thought. My great-grandmother. What was it like for her, leaving her tribe to marry a white man, settle down to his ways? Had she ever completely settled? Was that why Todd clung so fiercely to his home, why he had resented it so deeply when his daughter had chosen to leave?

'That must have been quite an adventure—Powell's trip

down the river,' she observed, thinking of the Colorado rushing on its turbulent way through the clefts and gorges, its waters white with tumbling foam. 'Especially when no one had gone that way before—when they didn't have any idea what to expect.'

Todd nodded. 'People said they were crazy. And Powell himself had only one arm—he rode in a chair fixed to his boat . . . They had some bad times, on that trip. Thought they were never going to get out alive. The party split up at one point, three of them decided to go it alone and walk out. They set off up one of the inner canyons and were never seen again. Killed by Indians, maybe, or caught in a flash flood—get a rainstorm up there and some of these canyons can be death-traps. But Powell and the rest of them made it. And now—why, it's a holiday trip.'

'You must have seen quite a few changes,' Tessa observed.

'Sure I have. There wasn't too much here when I was a youngster. The railroad was here—they started that in about 1901. I used to go down to the Santa Fe Station and watch the locomotives.'

Tessa imagined the boy, watching trains on the Rim just like any boy the world over. Wherever there were trains, she thought, there were small boys to watch them.

After that, Todd seemed to relax a little in his attitude towards her. Only a little, and it seemed that he looked at her sometimes as if he were struggling to release words, feelings, that could not be set free. She wished desperately that she could help him, knowing that already she was growing fond of this strange, difficult old man. His irascibility, she thought, was a shield he had erected years ago to protect himself from further pain—a shield too firmly in place to be dislodged now. Perhaps one day—if she stayed long enough, tried hard enough—it could be swept aside and he could break free of the cage he had built around himself. But Tessa, watching the lined face, knew that there might not be enough time left.

All the same, their talks became easier and more frequent. And only two or three nights later, Todd began to talk about Crane.

'Don't suppose he's told you much about himself,' he started, filling his pipe with tobacco.

'Not a lot,' Tessa said cautiously. 'I know he was adopted, of course, by Joe and Willa. And he did tell me how they died.' It was the first time she'd dared to mention Todd's son. 'I was sorry to hear about that, Grandfather,' she added quietly.

Todd grunted. Clearly, he didn't want to talk about Joe and Willa now—perhaps the subject was still too painful.

'It was pretty bad for Crane, that time,' he allowed. 'But you don't need me to tell you that. Anyone with any sense could see what it'd be like for a kid to lose a second set of parents—especially when they were so much better'n the first lot.'

Tessa looked at him. He was gazing towards the river, his face as brown and creased as old leather. Not sure whether he wanted her to speak, she said tentatively, 'Do you—does Crane know much about his first parents?'

Todd snorted. 'Too much, I'd say. Couple should never have had wed. Girl was half Indian—her pa came from the same tribe as my mother. Though they weren't related by blood, not any more'n most. Would have been all right— not a bad girl at all—and then she met this guy from the East. Wouldn't listen to any advice— she just had to have him. And then, o' course, after a few years it all split up; he went back East, and instead of sittin' it out here and lookin' after the boy—Crane—she went off after him.'

'Taking Crane with her? But then why——'

'No, she didn't take Crane with her. That was just it. Said nothin' mattered to her like this Easterner she'd wed, and she was going to stick with him, wherever he went. And if he didn't want the kid—neither did she.' Todd sucked angrily on his pipe, then turned his dark eyes on his granddaughter, 'Left him behind, she did—in an orphanage. She might just as well have chucked him on a garbage-heap. That's all he was, to her.'

Tessa stared at him, horrified, picturing the small boy, bewildered, abandoned among strangers—knowing that neither of his parents wanted him . . .

'But that's terrible,' she said softly. 'And then—after finding people who did care—to lose them too . . . No wonder——'

'No wonder Crane don't have much time for love and marriage?' Todd gave a short laugh. 'You've got it! But I wouldn't say anything to Crane about it—it's not a subject he likes to talk about.' He hauled himself from his chair. 'Well, guess that symphony's just about to finish. I'm turning in. You stay out here a bit longer if you like—guess you might have a bit of thinking to do.'

He went inside and Tessa sat listening to his movements, the sound of plates and cups being set out for tomorrow's breakfast, papers being picked up and moved, the recorder being switched off. The silence was suddenly deep. Somewhere she could hear the eerie call of a coyote and there was a rustling in the bushes near the stream—a mule deer, perhaps, or a bobcat.

The little story haunted her mind. It explained so

much—Crane's cynical attitude towards love, the traumas
that must have beset him since childhood. And not only
that—it explained Todd's own attitude to her mother's
marriage. How, after seeing what had happened to Crane's
real parents, he must have feared for his own daughter's
happiness. How helpless he must have felt when she went to
the other side of the world.

Tess sighed; had he ever really told her *why* he was so
against her marriage—or had he simply forbidden it and
expected her to accept his ruling? And had her mother ever
really wondered whether he had good reason for his
attitude, or had she merely rebelled against it, thinking it
was another example of his over-protectiveness?'

Perhaps she and Crane ought to learn from the mistakes
of their elders, she thought wryly. Make sure there were no
misunderstandings—be entirely honest with each other,
however painful or humiliating it might be.

But that was something that was easier said than done.
Already, Todd had warned her against discussing Crane's
past with him. And their relationship was still too
uncertain, too prickly, to tread such dangerous ground.

Tessa stared up at the night sky, watching the flickering
stars. Was Crane watching those same stars? Was he
thinking about her, down here, so far from the noise and
bustle of the 'real' world?

She sighed and acknowledged that he probably was not.
And wondered sadly why, when they spent so much time at
loggerheads, she should be missing him so much now . . .

The days passed quickly. Tessa, learning to look after the
hens, to tend the garden and to fish in the creek, found
herself more and more in tune with the Canyon. She felt as

if her life in Sussex were a dream, as if she had always lived here, among these towering red rocks, within sight of the massive inner ranges, her ears filled with the mocking calls of pinyon jays, the chatter of chipmunks, the roaring of the cascades. Wandering back from the creek, she stopped to watch a flight of violet-green swallows, marvelling at their whiplash movements through the clear air. There were swallows at home too, she remembered, and felt a sudden pang of guilt, as if by her delight in these birds she was betraying the place where she belonged.

But didn't she belong just as much to this wild, majestic canyon as to the soft woods and meadows of Sussex? Half her ancestry was here; was there any way she could deny it? Was there any reason why she should?

Thoughtfully, she rounded the last bend in the trail and came within sight of the long, low cabin. In the past few days, it had become home to her, and her grandfather—stubborn, hard to know, often brusque and cantankerous—a part of her life. Whatever happened, whether or nor she was ever able to talk to him about her mother, she would never forget him, never lose touch. And, by the same token, neither was she ever going to forget Crane.

It was as the last thought came into her mind that she caught sight of the helicopter standing on the grass behind the house.

A *helicopter*? She stared, hardly able to believe her eyes. It must—surely it could only be—Crane. He must have come back. Yet—if he could come by helicopter, why——? Unconsciously, she quickened her steps, feeling a sudden kick of her heart. Her colour rose, her eyes brightened, and without thinking she ran a hand through her tousled black hair.

'Crane!' she exclaimed as she came near and saw a shadow move in the darkness of the doorway. 'I didn't think you'd be back so soon! How . . .?'

Her words died. The figure in the doorway wasn't Crane at all. It wasn't even a man: it was a girl—a tall, blonde, tanned girl with laughing blue eyes who had stepped forward into the sunshine and was smiling at her. Tessa stopped abruptly, warning bells sounding somewhere inside. The girl looked warmly welcoming—but who was she, to welcome Tessa to her own grandfather's house? And behind that smile there was a distinctly speculative look— as if she were sizing Tessa up, assessing her—for what?

More slowly now, Tessa moved forward again, arriving at the veranda steps just as the girl came down.

She was tall, too—taller than Tessa—and although slim she was magnificently in proportion, with full breasts and a narrow waist. Her hips were full too, without being too wide, tapering into long, slender legs, all shown off to perfection by the beautifully cut green slacks and shirt she wore, and which Tess now recognised as a Park Ranger's uniform.

'So you're Tessa!' The voice was as warm and full of laughter as the sparkling eyes and generous mouth. 'I've been just longing to meet you. Crane's told me so much——' She stopped as if she said more than she meant to, and Tessa waited coolly, convinced that this girl never said a word she hadn't carefully thought out first. So Crane had told her all about Tessa, had he?'

All? she thought with a sudden surge of heat. And remembered the thoughts that taunted her at night—the thoughts of Crane with another woman. Thoughts that ought, surely, to mean nothing to her at all.

'Yes, I'm Tessa, she said at last, realising that the silence had gone on just a fraction too long. 'I'm afraid I haven't any idea who you are, though. Crane never mentioned——'

'Didn't he, though?' The blonde gave her an amused glance. 'The secretive devil! Well, I'm Natalee Wade. Crane and I've been friends for—oh, I don't know how long. I even remember your mother!'

Tessa's eyes widened in surprise. *This* girl had known her mother?

'I was only tiny, of course,' Natalee went on. 'Just about four years old when she ... went away. But I remember her, just.' Natalee tilted her head to one side, giving Tessa what was now a frankly assessing stare. 'You're like her, aren't you? Must have been quite a shock for poor old Todd when you turned up.'

Poor old Todd? Instinctively, Tessa glanced up at the house, wondering if he were within earshot. But there was no sound from inside, and Natalee laughed.

'It's OK, he can't hear us, I'd never dare call him "poor old Todd" if he could. He's up by the spring, getting water. I was just going to go and help when I saw you coming along.'

'When did you arrive?' It wasn't what she really wanted to know—which was why had Natalee come at all, and how well did she know Crane—but it had to do as a start.

'Oh, an hour or so ago. I expect you've realised I'm a Ranger. I'm down here on a photographic mission—I give shows in the Visitor Centre of slides I take. Crane and Emery flew me down . . .' She gave Tess a quick smile. 'And when he told me you were here—well, I couldn't resist having a look, could I?'

So Crane was here, too. Tessa glanced round involuntarily.

'They're all up at the spring,' Natalee explained, giving Tessa another smile. Tessa looked at her warily but the other girl's frankness was disarming and she couldn't help smiling in return. She still wasn't too sure of Natalee—she was slightly daunted by the bouncy confidence radiated by the American girl. But perhaps that was just her professionalism—Rangers had to deal with people all the time. And nothing she had said so far had been anything but friendly, although Tessa had been startled by the mention of her mother. Nobody else had so much as referred to her.

Briefly, she wondered how Crane managed to retain his cynicism in the face of Natalee's sunny openness.

After a quick snack and a drink, Emery flew back to the Rim, leaving Crane and Natalee behind. Tessa, feeling oddly awkward with Crane, stayed in the background, listening to their friendly banter and relaxed talk. Clearly the three of them—Todd, Crane and Natalee—had spent a good deal of time in each other's company and knew each other well. How well? Tessa wondered, watching Crane's face and noticing that the craggy furrows had been ironed out, leaving him looking younger than she had yet seen him. Just what was the relationship between him and the glowing, confident Park Ranger?

With Natalee in the house, everything changed. The American girl was a whirlwind of efficiency, taking charge the moment she arrived. When Tessa had come back from the creek, she had been tidying the big living-room. Papers had been stacked in tidy bundles or put away in drawers, books returned to their shelves, cassettes tucked out of sight in their boxes. Magazines had disappeared entirely, to be discovered later in a cupboard, piled methodically in chronological order. The hearth, scattered with twigs from the last fire, had been swept and a new fire laid, with the logs piled in a neat pyramid. The kitchen end of the room was shining.

The cheerful muddle in which Todd normally lived, and which Tessa had not liked to disturb—and in any case rather enjoyed—had vanished. Without it, the room looked different—more spacious, more orderly, yet somehow stark, as if the heart had been taken away from it.

'That's a whole lot better,' Natalee said, moving briskly about as she prepared their supper—she had refused Tessa's offer of help, saying that since she knew where everything was it was quicker to do it herself. 'Besides, you'll want to talk to your grandpa,' she added, as if Tessa were a small child. She almost shooed Tessa from the kitchen. 'You get out in the fresh air and I'll call you both when it's ready. And if Crane's still down at the creek, make him come straight in when he gets back—I'm waiting for those fish he promised us!'

Tessa found her grandfather sitting on the veranda, smoking his pipe gloomily. She smiled at him and settled into her usual chair.

Todd took his pipe from his mouth. 'She still in there?'

Tessa nodded. 'She's getting supper ready.'

'Thought so,' he said, and put his pipe back into his mouth.

Tessa smiled and stretched her arms above her head.

'What a lovely day it's been. I saw some violet-green swallows down by the creek—did I tell you? And some of those birds you said fly with them——'

'White-throated swifts.'

'Yes, that's right. And a huge bird overhead—an eagle of some kind, I think—black, with white underneath its wings——'

'That'd be a turkey vulture. They come in the spring.' Todd glanced at her. 'You keep your eyes open, don't you? Interested in wildlife and such?'

'Yes, I always have been.' Tessa took a breath. 'My father used to take me out into the woods a lot, showing me things, teaching me about the birds and animals. It's very different here, of course—that's what makes it so fascinating.'

'Hm.' Todd smoked for a few more moments in silence, and Tessa wondered if he was going to show any reaction to the mention of her father. He must have known him—it went without saying, of course, and yet until now she'd never consciously realised that they'd met, presumably known each other quite well. Had they got on? Or had Todd hated him from the beginning? It seemed hard to imagine, when she could remember her father as a kind, infinitely patient man who was liked by everyone.

'We've always spent a lot of time in the country,' she went on tentatively. 'Walks, picnics—looking for mushrooms and blackberries in the autumn, primroses and violets in the spring . . . We didn't pick them—Mum and Dad both liked to see them growing. But we used to bring home great sprays of leaves and mix them with our own garden flowers. Mum loved gardening.'

'Doesn't she now?' The question took her by surprise. She had been expecting Todd to get up and go inside, leave her as he had before when she'd brought up the subject of her home life. But it had been barked at her as if erupting from his lips, a question that had surprised Todd as much as it had her.

'She would do,' Tessa answered quietly. 'But she's ill. I told you in my letter.'

There was a long, heavy silence. Tessa glanced up through her lashes at the old man, sitting so near her, yet so far away in his thoughts. Was he going to say any more? Was he going to face up to the fact of his daughter's existence—a fact he'd been trying to avoid even with Tessa herself here to remind him? Or was he going to continue to close his mind and his heart against her—against them both?

Tessa scarcely dared to breathe. All her senses were vibrating with the tension. It was, she knew, a moment of crisis. Todd's reaction, at this moment, was crucial.

'I just wanted to come and see you,' she said, trying to keep her voice steady. 'And my mother wanted me to come—to talk to you before——' Her voice faltered.

'Before what?'

Todd's tone was unemotional, blank of all feeling, as if he'd switched off, wasn't interested. It was a tone that had deterred her in their previous conversations, but now Tessa determined not to let it affect her. This was something that had to be said, some time, and she might not get another chance, even though it wasn't at all easy to say.

She took a deep breath and plunged.

'Before she dies,' she said in a low voice. 'I told you she was ill. She hasn't very long to live, they say. And she wanted——' her voice shook now '——so much to know that you'd forgiven her.' Piteously, she lifted her small face, raising her eyes to his. 'Isn't there any chance at all?'

Todd didn't answer directly. There was silence from the

house now; even the birds outside had stopped singing. It was as if the entire Canyon were holding its breath.

'Forgiven her.' Todd said at last, slowly. 'I don't know. I don't really know what forgiveness is—how you go about it, when what's happened is half a lifetime ago, when the bitterness of it's eaten into your soul so deep . . . Some scars don't heal, girl, they show for the rest of your life . . .' He smoked his pipe in silence for a while, then spoke again. 'Tell me this . . . was she ever sorry she went away? Ever sorry she married your pa?'

Again, Tessa felt instinctively that this was no time for pretence. Whatever the consequences, honesty was the only thing there could be between herself and her grandfather.

'No, I don't think she was. Oh, life wasn't easy—Dad had to start again, more or less, when they went back to England, and when he died there wasn't any money to speak of, just enough to buy the house we lived in. And Mum was never strong, even before she got really ill.' Again, her voice shook. 'But no, I don't believe she ever regretted it. Only the rift it caused between you. She loved Dad always, and they were happy together. We were a happy family.'

'Well,' Todd said, taking the pipe from his mouth and appearing to address the sky, 'that's something, anyway.'

'How long are you staying?' Tessa asked casually—maybe a little too casually?—the next afternoon.

Natalee's smile flashed at her gaily. 'You want to get rid of me?'

'No—no, of course not—I just wondered—well, you said it was a sort of working trip and——'

'Oh, the photography.' The blonde head shimmered in the sun as Natalee nodded. 'Why yes, that's primarily why I'm here. And I guess you're wondering why I haven't been out today, snapping away at the flowers and the butterflies, hmm?' The laugh pealed through the still air. 'Well, it's night photography that I've come for this time. And we'll be out tonight, taking a few preliminary shots.'

'We?'

'Sure. Oh, don't look like that, Tessa. You know, you're too English for words?' Again the flashing smile and the laugh, while Tessa wondered crossly just what the other girl meant—how had she been looking, and why was it 'too English for words'? But Natalee was going on, her voice shaking with laughter. 'You think I ought to be *awfully, awfully proper*——' she gave the word a mock-English pronunciation '—and have a girl to help me, or d'you think if there's a man involved he's always got to be in charge? We know about liberation here, you know—we invented it! Even Crane, gorgeous hunk though he is, understands that.'

'Crane? You mean *Crane's* your assistant?'

'Sure, why not?' Natalee gave her a challenging glance. 'He's great. Knows the Canyon like the back of his hand—you need that when you're around in it at night.' Her lips twitched and she laughed again, a peal of gaiety that rang out and echoed against the rocky walls. 'There's no need to look so startled, Tessa! Can *you* think of anyone better to roam round the Canyon with at night than Crane Mellor?'

Tessa stared at her. Her emotions were tumbling inside her, a welter of confusion. Crane and Natalee, wandering in the Canyon at night—why did the images her mind insisted on conjuring up have such an effect on her? What was so unusual about it? After all, as Natalee said, they were living in the age of women's liberation now. You didn't have to have a chaperon with you wherever you went—that was back in the past. Men and women shared their lives to a much greater degree. They could even share a flat, a house, without others immediately suspecting an affair.

So why, when she heard the plans Natalee outlined so blithely, did she feel so disturbed? What did it matter to her what they did?

Tessa wondered the same thing again that night, when Crane and Natalee had returned from their preliminary walk. It had been highly successful, they'd told her and Todd, stowing away their gear. Natalee had taken a few shots and they ought to be good. Next night, they'd stay out till dawn.

'I'm surprised you can spare the time,' Tessa said to Crane, wishing her voice wouldn't sound so stiff. 'Didn't you tell me you had a business to run?'

Crane refilled his coffee mug and brought it over to the sofa, sitting down beside Natalee.

'Well, business isn't too brisk just now—it's that quiet, in-between period at the moment—and Emery can manage on his own. And there's nothing like a bit of night-hiking in the Canyon to tempt me down. It's got a special kind of magic then—right, Tessa?' His oblique glance took in Tessa's suddenly flaming face and he added smoothly, 'I'll bet Grandpa's already taken you and shown you some of his favourite spots.'

'Not at night, no.' Tessa looked at him, mutely begging him not to make a fool of her in front of Natalee, not to remind her of the night when she had stood in his arms and almost fallen with the storm of desire that had swept her.

'Then we'll have to put that right, won't we?' Crane said easily. 'Maybe you could come out with Nat and me one night. There's plenty of time—I can spend a week or so down here now. That enough for you, Natalee?'

'Fine.' The American girl's voice was warm and throaty. 'But what about Tessa? You'll be wanting to go back before then, won't you?'

'Me?' Startled, Tessa looked at Crane, then at her grandfather, still smoking his pipe and watching them all speculatively. 'I hadn't really thought about it—I hadn't made any plans.' She floundered to a halt, aware suddenly that she didn't want to leave Crane and this girl down here together. Aware that she didn't want to leave Crane . . . full stop. And neither did she want to leave her grandfather— not yet. Not just when they were beginning to know each other. Not now that they could talk.

We're family, she thought, the three of us. And I want us to be together—just for a little while, before it all comes to an end and I have to go. We've so little time . . .

'I'm sure someone will be passing who can see you on your way before Crane and I go back,' Natalee was saying now. 'One of the other Rangers will be going by in a day or two. I can give him a call if you like.'

Tessa looked at Crane. His expression was impassive, his face like weathered teak. His agate eyes told her nothing.

He wants me to go, she thought miserably, and wondered again why it should matter.

'I'll call him first thing,' Natalee said cheerfully. 'After all, you've been here several days—that's enough for most visitors, first time. And now I think——'

Todd shifted in his chair. He leaned forwards and

knocked out his pipe, and they all turned to look at him.

'Just a minute, before you get things too arranged.' His voice was slow, the cracks of age making it gruff, but it still held a considerable authority. 'No one's asked me what *I* think Tessa should do—or what I might want her to do.' The dark eyes, still bright, surveyed them. 'Tessa and me have got a lot of catching up to do,' he said laconically. 'I reckon we need a mite longer'n a few days to do it in. Could be we need a few weeks—even months, if Tessa cares to stay that long. Anyway, what I'm sayin' is she needn't be in any hurry to go. She can stay with her old Grandpa as long as she wants—that suit you, girl?'

Tessa felt her eyes mist with tears. She looked at Todd and nodded, unable to speak. And then she caught Crane's glance and her heart leaped.

For the first time since she had known him, Crane's guard was completely down. His face was no longer shuttered, his eyes no longer veiled. The bitter lines had gone, leaving a tenderness that caught her breath in her throat. And in the agate eyes was a glow that took her straight to his heart.

For a moment, they gazed at each other. The room, the other occupants, faded; there were only the two of them. And in that moment of revelation, Tessa saw clearly, as if in a slash of lightning across a darkened sky, just what had been happening to her.

All this time—perhaps from the moment they had met, certainly from soon afterwards—she had been falling in love with him. With Crane, who had shown so clearly that he had no time for her. Crane Mellor, who had held her in his arms and woken fires that she had never dreamed smouldered in her heart; who had woken her body and all its desires with one caressing glance.

No wonder she had responded so ardently. No wonder she missed him so desperately by day, ached for him at night. No wonder he was never out of her thoughts, a constant yearning that was with her even in her dreams.

A log shifted in the fire Todd had lit, and Tessa turned her head, dazed, seeing the room as if she had just returned after a long journey. The moment of elation, of ecstasy, passed and was replaced by a deep, desperate longing that was worse than any pain she had felt yet.

For she knew, quite clearly, that her love could never be returned. Crane's expression had not—could not—have been one of love, merely an acknowledgement of her success with her grandfather. His concern had always been with Todd—he was simply telling her that he was glad she had succeeded in not hurting the old man.

He would never love her, because he would never love anybody. The traumas of his childhood, the bitterness that had hardened around him, would not allow him to soften that far. An affair, yes—he'd already proved his virility. But even the tenderest of his kisses, as he'd taken pains to point out, had been meaningless—just a way of passing time, a pleasure to be taken where it could be found.

Giving love to Crane Mellor would, she knew, be like dropping it into a bottomless pit. But that didn't make it possible to stop. Now that she had recognised the cause of the turmoil within her, Tessa knew that it was something she was going to have to live with for the rest of her life. A yearning pain that could never be relieved.

And going back to Sussex wasn't going to be any help at all. Distance could only make it worse.

CHAPTER SEVEN

AFTER a wakeful night, Tessa finally dozed off at around sunrise, and then slept heavily until ten. She awoke to find Natalee's bed empty and, when she went into the big living-room, nobody about.

Coffee was the first requirement, and the warm aroma cleared her head a little. She shuddered at the thought of food, taking the pot and a mug out to the veranda and settling herself there to stare out across the valley as she drank.

Sleep seemed to have done little to sort out the tumbled sensations of the night before. Once again, helpless in the grip of her confused emotions, Tessa thought over the events and tried to make sense of them. But was there any sense to be made? She shook her head wearily, her eyes fixed unseeingly on the green valley. The sound of cascading water, from the springs which erupted from the canyon walls, filled her ears, while nearer the hens scratched contentedly for the corn Todd had thrown on the ground and the mules grazed lazily in the fenced-off pasture.

But Tessa was aware of none of these things. In her mind, she was back in the darkness of the night, her mind reeling with the shock of that moment of revelation—the blinding realisation that she loved Crane.

A groan escaped her lips. How on earth could it have happened? *When* had it happened? When they had walked here in the Canyon the night before he'd gone back to the

Rim, and he'd held her in his arms and kissed her with such urgency? Or as they'd lain together in their sleeping-bags, waking to experience the breathlessness of dawn, and he'd touched her face with such tenderness? Or—and her face still flamed scarlet at the memory—when they'd encountered each other, naked, in the pool?

Or was it none of these times? Perhaps they were simply an expression of what had been there all the time. Perhaps she had actually fallen in love with him as they rode down the trail, bumping uncomfortably on the backs of the mules. Or even before that—living in his house, waiting for him to come back from the airfield, writing letters to her mother, miserably aware that Crane didn't want her there.

Frustrated, she shook her head and poured some more coffee. She would never know how, where or when it had happened. If she had—she could have prevented it, drawn back before the damage was done. Or had it been as inevitable as it was irrevocable?

Because she knew that now it had happened—now that she was in love with Crane—there would be no going back. It was something that would stay with her for life.

And that was nothing but bad news. For she knew all too well that Crane felt nothing for her. He had made that perfectly clear. Their physical encounters, shattering though she had found them, were nothing more than the effects of the Canyon and its mystery, drawing out their most primitive instincts. And he had told her quite positively of his attitude to love itself. For Crane Mellor, it didn't exist.

'Well, there you are! The sleeping beauty—awake at last, huh?'

Tessa jerked round, spilling coffee on the wooden floor of the veranda. There was no need to look to see who was there—Crane's deep, drawling tones were already sending a shiver down her spine. She stared at him, mesmerised.

Crane was leaning casually against the door-jamb. He was dressed entirely in black—close-fitting black jeans that revealed the outlines of his powerful thighs, and a shirt that was open at the neck to expose a deeply tanned chest. The colour intensified the darkness of his hair, as black as the shadows of night, and the tiger's eyes that watched her so closely that Tessa felt agonisingly sure that he could read her mind.

'I thought you'd all gone off somewhere,' she said breathlessly.

Crane shrugged. 'I came back for some equipment. Natalee wanted to explore a cave up in Labyrinth Canyon and we didn't have a torch or any flash gear.'

'Labyrinth Canyon?' Tessa had heard Todd speak of it, but she had not yet been there. It hadn't sounded too appealing—dark and twisting, Todd had told her, its floor so narrow between sheer black cliffs that no sun ever penetrated there. 'Is Todd there too?'

'Sure. He loves showing off his canyons—you should know that by now.' Crane's smile glimmered down at her for an instant, lightening the sombre darkness of his face, and she caught a glimpse of the man he could be if only he had never given way to cynicism. 'Anyway, now you're around, why don't you come along too?'

Tessa hesitated. Todd might be pleased to see her, but would Natalee? And then she scolded herself. What did it matter what Natalee thought—it was Todd who mattered, wasn't it? And he'd made it quite clear last night that he wanted her to stay.

And, painful though it might be, it would mean a little longer with Crane.

'Yes,' she said, swinging her legs over the side of the long chair and stretching herself upright, 'Yes, I'll come. I'd like to see Labyrinth Canyon.'

She looked up at Crane, a sudden smile curving her lips. For no reason, the morning seemed suddenly lighter and all at once she was aware of the colours of trees, shrubs, flowers, and the sound of the tumbling water, the birds singing and the soft clucking of the hens. Beauty was all around, she thought with a flood of pure happiness, and when one of the mules gave a snorting bray, she laughed.

Crane stared at her, his eyes darkening, a glimmer of flame somewhere in their depths; twin fires ready to ignite. With a catch of her breath, Tessa's laughter died, and she remained quite still, transfixed.

'Do that again,' he said in a low voice.

'Do what?' Her words were husky, almost lost in the sudden beating of her heart.

'Laugh like that. As if—as if the whole world had suddenly told you a joke. As if you——' He stopped.

'As if I—what?' Tessa prompted, half afraid of the answer, and when he shook his head and didn't answer, she went on more boldly, 'I don't know why I laughed, Crane, except that—well, suddenly, everything seemed so perfect. As if, like you say, the world told me a joke, and it was the best I'd ever heard. Maybe for an instant that's what happened. Maybe for just a split second everything bad stopped, there was no fighting or misery or pain anywhere in the world, and the joy of it got through to me.' She stopped, embarrassed, but as she turned away Crane caught at her arm, and the shock ran through her body like fire.

'I told you the other night,' he muttered, drawing her close to him, 'the Canyon has some strange effects on people. But I've never known it affect me the way it does when we're together.' Almost unwillingly, as if forced by something greater than himself, he bent his head and laid his lips on hers. 'What does it mean, Tess, can you tell me that?' He whispered, and then they were both lost in the kiss.

Tessa stood in his arms, held close by his firm embrace. Her mind sang with joy, her body pulsated with the love that surged through her as inexorably as waves beating on a distant shore. Knowing that she loved him gave a completely new dimension to the sensations she was experiencing now, and she abandoned herself rapturously to the responses that had terrified her before, giving her lips with a tender passion that filled her with wonder.

'Tessa!' he said, and a groan tore its way up from his throat as he gathered her more closely, his arms and lips suddenly fierce with desire. With a leap of excitement, Tessa opened her mouth to his, welcoming the urgent exploration of his tongue, letting her lips mould to his mouth, as she moulded her body against him, her softness crushed willingly against the ruthless muscularity of his maleness. Her hands had found their way up his back now, fingers stroking his powerful neck, tangling in the thick hair. And when she opened her eyes for a fraction of a second, she was shaken still further by the expression on his face—an expression of desperate longing, as if he knew, even as he kissed and held her, that his yearning could never be assuaged.

'Tessa—tell me to stop,' he muttered thickly, his hands moving strongly over her body, covering her breasts, fingers forcing aside the thin blouse that was all that covered them. 'I've lost my senses . . . Tessa, help me . . .' He bent his head again, running his tongue over the nipples he had just exposed, grunting with satisfaction as they tightened under his lips, the breasts swelling against him. 'God, you're so beautiful . . .'

For a few moments, Tessa lay back in his arms, body arched against him, as aware of every tiny point of contact between them as if her nerves had been sharpened, honed to the finest degree of sensitivity. Her body clamoured for full release, the fulfilment she knew Crane desired so passionately too, and briefly, aware that she was playing with fire, she allowed herself to imagine that it was going to happen—here and now, in the sunlight of the valley, with only the birds, the hens and her brown mule as witnesses.

And then, as Crane's hands began to move again, caressing her body with a sure and purposeful expertise, she knew that the dream was over. She and he were not going to make love here, in this bright valley on the floor of the Grand Canyon. They weren't going to make love anywhere; because whatever she felt for Crane, his own emotion was no more than a passing madness. And if he were to give in to it, she knew instinctively that he would never forgive himself.

With a sudden slash of pain, intense as white lightning, Tessa thought of Natalee. What the relationship really was between the blonde American girl and Crane, she had no way of knowing—but she could make plenty of guesses. And they all led to the same heart-sinking conclusion.

From every word that they spoke, every glance they exchanged, it was clear that Crane and Natalee were on close—*intimate*—terms. How could anyone not believe that they were lovers—that Crane had on many, many occasions, held that voluptuous body in his arms, buried his face in the shower of sun-gold hair, made the glowing face burn with his kisses?

He wouldn't have needed the influence of the Grand

Canyon to stir his desire for Natalee, Tessa thought bitterly. And perhaps it wasn't even that so-called influence which had driven him into her own arms—but nothing more than ordinary frustration at having been parted from the woman he loved. It wasn't Tessa who roused him at all—it was Natalee, and even now Tessa was no more than a substitute.

Facing it was a pain that seared Tessa right through to her soul. But even in the midst of her torment, she knew that not facing it could cause an even worse agony. And having acknowledged what she felt sure to be the truth, there was only one course left to her.

His fingers were trailing down her body, hardly touching her bare skin as they skimmed over her waist. Tessa caught her breath. If she didn't stop him now, there would be no going back ... With a quick movement, knowing that it had to be done, she twisted out of his arms and backed away against the veranda rail, panting, breathless and feeling as though she had just thrown away something irreplaceably valuable.

Crane stood quite still. He was breathing heavily, his face dark, his eyes hooded.

'I'm sorry,' Tessa said, her hands tight on the rail behind her. 'You did ask me to stop you ... I had to.'

Her eyes were huge in her pale face as she stared up at him, all her emotions naked for him to read; but Crane wasn't looking into them now. He had already turned away, moving to the other end of the veranda, passing a hand shakily through the ruffled black hair that only moments earlier had been tangled through her own fingers. He came to a halt at the corner, his hands on the rail as he stared out along the valley.

Maybe he'd been afraid Natalee would come back and

catch them together, Tessa thought ruefully. But there was no sign of the other girl and her breath coming more easily now, she attempted to ease the tension that still crackled between them.

'Shall I bring some food?' she asked, her voice husky. 'Bread—cheese—something to drink? Or did you take stuff with you?'

Slowly, Crane turned. From the other end of the veranda, he stared at her, and even at that distance she could still feel the shock of the naked emotion that blazed from his eyes. Involuntarily, she took a step back, and as she did so his face changed. As if a shutter had been dropped, the emotion vanished, leaving a mask that could have been carved from stone, lit by eyes that might have been pieces of coal.

'Food?' he said, as if it were a new idea to him. 'Oh, yeah, sure, bring along some food. We took some, but I don't think Natalee was planning on your joining us.' I bet she wasn't, Tessa thought wryly. 'I'll go and fetch that flash gear,' Crane added, and disappeared inside the house.

Well! So that was that. Another little episode that was over almost as soon as it had begun, leaving her own emotions a little more raw, a little more bruised than before. And yet—could she be sorry that it had happened? When all too soon she would be back in Sussex, with only a few memories to carry her through the rest of her life?

As she went to collect her food, Tessa faced the fact that she was now unlikely ever to love another man.

Labyrinth Canyon was, as Tessa had expected, a heavily shadowed and gloomy crevice in the glowering rocks. Nothing grew there, and the smoothness of the boulders suggested that water had poured through with some violence over a considerable period. When she remarked on this to Crane, he nodded.

'Get a lot of rain topside and it all surges out of the springs in the Canyon walls. Filters down through the limestone at the top, you see, and then comes out when it meets non-porous rock lower down. And if there's a heavy storm—well, it can be real dangerous, a sudden flash flood that brings down rock and mud and trees and anything standing in its way. You want to be clear of the side canyons when that happens. Look at the water-line up there. You can see the height it can rise to.'

Tessa followed his pointing finger and shivered. The water-line, a clear distinction between the smooth, worn boulders and the rough cragginess above, was about twelve feet above her head. She could well believe that to be caught here in a flash flood would mean almost certain death.

'But how do you know if there's a storm up on the Rim?' she asked nervously. 'It might be all over by the time you realised, and too late to get out.'

'There's always that chance,' Crane admitted cheerfully. 'But it looks pretty clear now. Don't worry—a storm up above generally penetrates to the floor as well, and you get plenty of warning. But when the sky's as blue as it is today, there's not much danger.'

Slightly comforted, Tessa followed him through the twisting gullies. It was too narrow now to walk side by side, and she found herself staring warily up at the great slabs of rock on either side, wondering if any of them were due to fall. Todd had told her that the Canyon was a living entity, still in the process of formation, and that it was changing subtly every day. Rocks fell for no apparent reason, forced away from their places—by erosion, by pressure, who could know? Somewhere that had been perfectly safe for a long as man had known the Canyon could become a death-trap overnight, and there was often no way of foreseeing it.

'It's just no use worrying about it,' he'd added, seeing her eyes widen. 'The Canyon's a big place, after all. We might not see any changes around here for generations. And life's never been all that certain.'

All the same, she thought now, as they squeezed past a boulder that appeared to be resting entirely on one tiny corner and held in place by little more than a pebble, if rocks were going to start falling anywhere, it would surely be somewhere like this, a narrow gorge where water frequently poured with such force that the walls were worn as smooth as a silk dress.

Crane glanced back, eyebrows lifted in enquiry. 'All right? Not scared?'

Tessa smiled back. If Natalee could come here without fear, she certainly wasn't going to show her own nervousness.

'Yes, I'm fine, thanks. It's fascinating.'

'Good.' He stopped and reached back for her hand. 'This next part's a bit tricky. Try not to look down.'

Try not to look down? Tessa's eyes immediately fell, and she stepped back with a gasp, unable to prevent the involuntary reaction.

Creeping round the huge bulge of a boulder that overhung the narrow path, she found herself facing what appeared to be a deep crack in the earth's surface, an abyss about six feet wide which dropped away into a blackness which seemed bottomless. From somewhere, echoing and uncanny, came the sound of rushing water. But there was nothing to be seen, and the only way of crossing the chasm was by a natural bridge of rock, less than eighteen inches wide, dangerously thin and worn in places, and with not so much as a single post by which to steady herself.

'I told you not to look down,' Crane said, and Tessa's panic turned to irritation.

'How could you expect me not to look? Am I supposed to follow blindfold wherever you lead?' She took another quick look at the gap which yawned blackly at her feet, and shuddered. 'I'm sorry—I don't think I can cross that.'

'Oh say, you're not going to run out on me now, are you?' His voice was pleasant but firm. He crossed the narrow bridge as casually as if it had been a garden path. 'Look, it's not so bad. You can walk across that as easy as crossing a room. Hold my hand.'

He came back to the middle of the bridge and held out a strong brown hand. Tessa eyed it doubtfully. Certainly, he had crossed easily enough—but no doubt he'd done it before, and he was used to these terrifying gaps. She peered yet again into the depths. How many people had fallen to their doom down there?

'Come on,' Crane said encouragingly, 'take hold. You trust me, don't you?'

An ironic question, she thought, but had to admit that in these circumstances she did. Crane wasn't the reckless type who would play with his own life or the lives of others. Even during that hair-raising flight through the Canyon, she'd known that he was completely in control. He wasn't going to take any chances now, either.

Cautiously, she stretched out her hand and felt him enclose it in his, warmth and strength flowing from his fingers.

'Now,' he said quietly, and Tessa stepped carefully on to the bridge. 'That's it ... Again ... A little more.' He was backing away, regaining solid ground on his side of the crack. 'Two more steps and you're there. One more . . . And a bit . . . and that's it. Well done, Tessa!'

Breathless, laughing now with relief, Tessa flung herself across the last few inches and fell into Crane's arms. At once, they came around her, holding her tightly against him, and when she looked up she saw that his face was sombre. For a few moments they stayed quite still, so close that their hearts seemed to beat in unison, and then Crane let her go and Tessa stepped away.

'Right,' he said, turning away along the trail. 'We'd better get along. It's not much further now to the cave.'

Subdued, Tessa followed. Had Crane begun to realise the strength and nature of her feelings for him? She wondered, and hoped not. She wanted no more complications in their already strained relationship. As long as he thought her reactions were, like his, due to the effect of the Canyon and its mystery, she could cope. If he ever knew that she loved him . . . Her mind shook at the thought.

As for his reactions—Tessa was grateful to him for the control he had shown, even though it had sometimes threatened to break down. As she'd surmised earlier, his cynicism about love had done nothing to lessen his natural male desires, and might even have intensified them; failure to make a strong, loving relationship could have that effect, she imagined. She was thankful that some scruple had held him back from what for some men might have seemed a perfectly natural course to take—her seduction.

For a moment, she allowed herself to play with the idea of allowing—even encouraging—him to do just that. Wouldn't it be worth it, to be possessed by him just once, to express to the full all the love and need that was tearing her body apart? Just so that she had that one time to remember for the rest of her long, lonely life?

But even as she thought of it, she knew that she could never let it happen. Because Crane, whatever his faults, had a very high standard of behaviour. And if he once transgressed it, he would suffer and suffer deeply.

If I love him, Tessa thought sadly, I can't be responsible for that.

The canyon had opened out a little now, the narrowest part behind them, and she could see that it was running right up to the walls of the Grand Canyon itself. The multi-coloured bands of the mile-high cliffs rose sheer ahead of them, and at their feet she could see a dark, vertical shadow.

'That's the cave,' Crane said. 'And there are Grandpa and Natalee just outside it. They promised they wouldn't go inside until I got back with the torch and flash gear.'

As they came closer, Tessa caught a quickly concealed flash of pleasure on her grandfather's face. Well, at least one person's glad to see me, she thought with a lift to her spirits, and went forward ahead of Crane.

'Hello,' she said cheerfully. 'Sorry I overslept this morning. I was awake when Crane came back so I thought I'd come along too—I've been wanting to see Labyrinth Canyon.'

'I'm surprised you made it along there,' Natalee said. 'It's pretty hairy in places.'

'Oh, Crane helped me a lot.' Tess slipped her pack from her shoulders and sat down on the rock. 'Were you just about to eat? I'm starving—only had coffee before we set out.'

'Hm. Might as well eat now 'n' then go inside the cave after.' Todd settled himself on a rock nearby. 'Don't suppose you thought to put any of that coffee you made into a flask?'

'I did.' Triumphantly, Tess produced it and poured some out. 'There, try that. It's my best yet.' She turned to Natalee with a confiding grin. 'Todd said I couldn't make decent coffee when I came, so he's been teaching me. I'm going to give him a few lessons in tea-making after this.'

'Tea!' Todd snorted contemptuously, and Tessa laughed.

'I quite agree, the way you make it.' She unwrapped some bread and cheese. 'But I'll tell you one thing—I don't think I've ever tasted such good bread as you make, Grandfather. Unless——' She stopped suddenly, feeling cold and uncertain.

'Unless what?' Crane said quietly, and when Tessa looked up at him her eyes were filled with tears.

'Unless it's the bread Mum makes,' she whispered, and lowered her head.

The words fell into a silence that even Natalee didn't seem inclined to break. And Tessa wondered whether her mother had learned to bake bread from this wiry, tough old man who sat on a rock nine thousand miles away from his estranged daughter. And whether he was remembering it now.

Was she doing any good at all down here? she wondered yet again. Was she any nearer to reconciling the two?

And—whether or not she succeeded—at what cost were her efforts going to be to herself?

CHAPTER EIGHT

For the next few days, life at the cabin seemed to revolve around Natalee and her photography. It was part of her job, she explained to Tessa, and she would be making up a slide show to give at the Visitor Centre later on.

'The vast majority of people who come to Grand Canyon just stay up on the Rim, and never get down inside at all,' she said. 'Some of them aren't capable of making the hike, or taking a mule ride, some of them just don't enjoy that kind of thing. And a whole lot don't even stay long enough. Do you know, the average time a visitor spends at the Canyon is no more than three hours!'

'Is that all? But they can't possibly catch more than a glimpse in that time!'

Natalee shrugged. 'Well, that's what's been estimated. They come on bus trips, stop at Mather Point or Desert View, take some photos, have a look around, and then get back in their Greyhound and go on—to Vegas, or LA, or maybe one of the other National Parks—Zion, or Bryce or Death Valley. They don't have time to hang about on those trips.'

Tessa thought about it. 'I suppose it's a temptation, while you're here, to see as much as you can,' she said reflectively. 'But it seems a shame to gloss over such marvellous scenery. It must all be a blur when you get back home again. I think I'd rather just see one place and give it enough time to get to know it properly.'

144

'Well, you might need a lifetime or two to do that,' Natalee suggested drily, and the two girls laughed.

Tessa watched Natalee preparing her cameras. The American girl was certainly very efficient and thorough, and Tessa couldn't help feeling a liking for her. Natalee was what she thought of as typically American—blonde, beautiful in a statuesque way, radiating confidence and warm friendliness. Any tension between them was, she recognised, the kind that was bound to arise when there were two women in competition for the same man.

But were they in competition? Tessa turned away to stare across the valley. She loved Crane, deeply and irrevocably, she knew that now. Whether Natalee's feelings were as deep, she couldn't begin to guess. But it was Crane's response that was important—and although his response to Tessa was as fierce and as rapid as a bush fire taking hold, she knew that love wasn't a part of it.

No, there was no competition between herself and Natalee. If Natalee wanted Crane, she would have him, on terms that they both understood. And at least part of the blonde's easy assurance must come from that knowledge.

'When are you going to start your photography?' she asked now.

'Oh, tonight, I guess. There's not a lot of moon yet so we'll do the caves. That one up in Labyrinth is really something—I want to go back there first. Those bats nesting in the crevices! I must get some shots of them flying in and out—it'll look real eerie!'

It certainly would, Tessa thought, repressing a shiver. She hadn't enjoyed the trip into Labyrinth Cave at all, finding it even gloomier and narrower than the canyon that led to it. She had been thankful to get out into the air again, even though the sunshine didn't penetrate between the dank walls, and had been quite unable to join in Natalee's exuberant delight.

'Well, I guess that's it.' Natalee finished her preparations and stood up. 'I'll just make some food to take with us, and then I guess we'll be on our way. We won't need to take much tonight—we're coming back tomorrow. But then we're going on a longer hike and we'll be away two or three days, so we'll need to take along quite a lot. Crane's a very hungry man!'

As Tessa watched them go away down the trail, her feelings were mixed. In a way, it was a relief to see them go and know that the days would return to their normal peaceful routine, with no Crane to set up tensions in her, and no Natalee to make them worse. But on the other hand, she knew she was going to be constantly thinking of them, out there in that disturbing darkness together ... constantly wondering what they were doing ...

To take her mind off them, she decided to concentrate on her grandfather. After all, he was the reason she was here, wasn't he? She spent the rest of the day with him, catching brown trout in the creek, helping with the hens and the mules, picking salad vegetables in the garden and watching as he showed her how to make bread.

'You say your ma makes bread still?' he asked as he kneaded, his strong brown hands working at the dough.

'Yes, quite often. She says she enjoys it—yeast dough's like a living thing. She can always tell if it isn't going to prove, it feels dull and heavy.'

He nodded. 'That's right. How come she hasn't taught you, then?'

'I don't really know. We keep meaning to have a session,

but we've never got around to it. There's always been so much else to do—school, college, exams.'

'You're a kind of secretary, that right?'

'Yes, a personal assistant. Only the boss I was working for got a new job abroad, and since I didn't get on with the man who was taking his place, I decided to have a change too. That's why I came out here now, I had some money saved and it seemed a good opportunity.'

'You told me Betsy was ill,' Todd said, his voice flat.

'Yes, she is.' Tessa took a breath. 'Very ill. It's her heart—they can't do much about it, and she won't consider a transplant. She says——' her voice shook '—says she's had her chance and there are others who need it more.'

'She says that?' Todd's fingers, working methodically in the dough as they talked, were still. 'I wonder what makes her feel that way?'

'I don't think she's ever been really happy since Dad died,' Tessa said quietly.

Todd stared at the brown mass in his hands. 'I guess this is ready to put to rise now.' His voice was expressionless. 'Let's have a bit of music. And then I reckon I'll be ready for bed.'

Tessa watched as he placed the dough in a cool place to spend the night rising; he would then shape it quickly into loaves and rolls early next morning, and it would be baked in time for breakfast. She wondered what he was thinking, but there was no hint in the seamed face and she settled down to listen to the music, aware that there was no point in re-opening the conversation. Todd would only let her talk about Betsy for so long at a time—and that in itself was an advance on his attitude when she had first arrived.

He played Beethoven's *Pastoral Symphony*, and as Tessa

listened she found herself transported out of the Grand Canyon and back to the fields and woods of her Sussex home. How was her mother now? she wondered. She hadn't heard since the day she had left Crane's house to come down into the Grand Canyon—over a week ago.

Perhaps tomorrow she could telephone Betsy and speak to her. Perhaps Todd himself might be persuaded to talk, too.

Next morning, however, Tessa forgot her resolution. She slept late and was woken by the smell of fresh bread. Hurriedly, she jumped out of bed and found Todd just setting the table for breakfast.

'You've baked it!' she exclaimed, gazing with pleasure at the fresh rolls that he was taking from the oven, their golden crusts steaming. 'It looks gorgeous and smells marvellous. I can't wait!'

'Give it a few minutes to settle itself,' Todd warned. 'And come on outside. I've got something to show you.'

Curious, Tessa followed him out and found him bending over something on the trail.

'It's a hoofmark,' she said.

'That's right. A hoofmark. And you know what kind of animal made that mark?'

Tessa shook her head.

'A bighorn sheep,' Todd said impressively. 'One of the rarest animals in the Canyon these days. There used to be plenty, but when the Canyon wasn't managed so well as it is now, they started to die out. We don't get a lot of them now, but when we do the Rangers like to know about it. Pity Natalee isn't here.'

'They'll be here soon though, won't they? Natalee said

they'd be coming back today.'

'That's right, she did. Then they're aiming to go off on the big hike later in the day.' Todd looked again at the hoofmark. 'Well, I guess we won't disturb this. We'll have our breakfast anyway—not much else we can do, until they come.'

They went back to the cabin and made coffee. When they were half-way through their meal, Tessa heard sounds from outside and got up to look.

'They're here.' She watched as Crane and Natalee came along the trail, feeling a sudden embarrassment. They'd spent the night together, after all—and had they occupied themselves simply with photography? Would it show in their faces? She hardly looked at Crane as he bent his head to come through the door.

'Hi, there.' Natalee clearly had no embarrassment at all. She was smiling broadly as she came in, and dumped her photographic gear on the big sofa with a sigh of relief. 'Is that coffee I smell? And new-baked bread—my, oh my! You certainly know how to welcome starving photographers, Todd!'

'Did you have a successful night?' Tessa asked, and could have bitten her tongue out.

Crane glanced at her sideways, his mouth twitching. 'Very successful indeed,' he said gravely. 'I think we can both say that, can't we, Natalee? It was a success from your point of view, wasn't it?'

'Oh, sure—wonderful.' Natalee carved off a chunk of bread and spread it with butter. 'This really is the best bread I've ever tasted. You're a marvel, Todd.'

'Even more than you think,' Todd remarked. 'We had a bighorn sheep past here some time during the night.'

Natalee paused, her bread half-way to her mouth. 'A bighorn? Are you sure?'

'I don't know any other animal makes those kind of marks. See for yourself—it's just outside.'

Natalee put down her bread and followed him, indicating to Crane to follow; but Crane didn't move. He grinned and shook his head, pouring himself some coffee as he did.

'You go. I'll look when I've had a drink.' He tipped up the mug and drank deeply. 'Whew, I needed that! And how have you been, Tessa?'

'Fine.' She wanted to say *you've only been gone a few hours*, but was all too aware of what those hours might have contained for him. 'Natalee's very excited about the sheep.'

'Well, a bighorn's something to get excited about. There used to be a lot of them around. Then men started to hunt the mountain lions, and that resulted in the *burros*—the wild donkey—over-populating the Canyon. They competed for the same foods, and the *burros* won. Now the lions aren't hunted any more, the *burros* are kept down and the bighorns are making a comeback, but it's a slow process and any natural disaster to them could wipe them out.'

'I see.' Tessa looked up as Todd and Natalee came back. Natalee was beaming, her eyes shining. Her spun-gold hair swung like a bell as she came over to Crane.

'It's a bighorn, right enough. The closest one's been to the trail in a long time. I ought to let them know up at the Centre.'

'Use the phone,' Crane said, but Todd shook his head.

'Out of action. I tried to phone through my grocery order yesterday and it wasn't working. Line failure somewhere, I guess. I'll give it another try now.'

He picked up the phone, and screwed up his mouth. 'No dice. It's not speaking to us today.'

'So what do we do?' Natalee appealed to Crane. 'I ought to let them know. Bruce especially—the bighorn's his baby and he'd want to come down, see if he can spot how many there are. Heck, I don't know what to do. I guess I ought to go back topside and let 'em know.'

'Don't forget we left some of your gear in Labyrinth,' Crane reminded her, and Natalee frowned with annoyance.

'Heck, so we did.' She turned to Tessa and her grandfather. 'We were going to go back tonight and do some more, so I left some of the gear here to save carrying it all ... I'll need it if we're going to see bighorn, but if I'm going topside I ought to set off right away. I don't know what I'd better do.'

'Well, I could go and get your gear from Labyrinth,' Crane said. 'Tessa'll come along to help carry—that OK, Tessa?'

'Well—yes, of course.' Tessa was startled at being drawn into this, and didn't fancy the idea of another trip into Labyrinth at all, but there was little she could say. Everyone else evidently considered this an important moment, and she wasn't going to be the one to make things difficult. 'And if we're all going to be shooting off in different directions, we'd better get equipped,' she went on, pulling herself together. 'Food—what a good job you made all that bread, Grandfather! And there's ham, and cheese, and fruit ... Natalee, maybe you could get some more supplies while you're on the Rim, and take in Grandfather's grocery order too. And—there's something else you could do. For me.'

'Sure—anything you want.' The American girl followed her to the kitchen. 'What is it, Tessa?'

Tessa faced her, speaking quietly so that the two men wouldn't hear. 'I'd like you to telephone England,' she said. 'I was hoping to do it myself today but with Grandfather's phone out of order, I can't. But it's a week since I heard from Mum and I'd like to know how she is. Would you do that?'

Natalee smiled warmly. 'Sure,' she said. 'I'll do that for you, Tessa. I'll be glad to.' She stood for a moment longer, looking at Tessa as if there were something more she wanted to say. Something about Crane . . .? And then the moment passed. Crane began to call out something about film and flashlights. Natalee nodded again and turned away, and Tessa began thankfully to pack bread, cheese and ham into various plastic boxes.

It seemed even darker today as she and Crane made their way through the twisting passages of Labyrinth Canyon. Tessa shivered. She would be glad when they had collected Natalee's gear and were back out in the main canyon, on their way to Cool Valley.

They had left the cabin later than they'd expected. Natalee had set off immediately, the trek to the Rim likely to take her all day, going as fast as was possible on the steep trail. She didn't really like to push it like that, she'd told Tessa, but the other Ranger, Bruce, would want to know about the bighorn as soon as possible.

Tessa waved her off and went back into the cabin. Todd was already tidying up and she helped him to bring some order back into the big living-room. Not that it was ever really tidy—but the homely disorder that Todd lived in was neatness itself compared with its condition now.

'Something about that girl,' Todd observed as he stacked Natalee's possesions in a corner. 'She likes to get everyone else organised but there are times when she needs a bit of organisation herself. I wouldn't say she'd left this place in a mess, exactly, but I reckon if the police were called in they'd say there were signs of a struggle.'

Tessa laughed. 'I think she was too excited about the bighorn sheep. She's generally very efficient.'

'Oh, sure,' he said, and something in his voice made Tessa glance at him.

'Don't you like Natalee?'

'I never said that,' he said quickly, and then grinned a little shamefacedly. 'Well ... since you ask ... I dunno. She's a nice enough girl, I guess, but—oh, well, she's a mite too efficient for me. A bit too managing. I dare say she'll improve.'

'Crane seems to get on well with her,' Tess said casually, and earned another sharp glance.

'Ah, that's so. They've been friends for a long time. I used to think they might be getting married one day. But now— I dunno.'

Tess's heart gave a leap. 'Don't you think it's likely now?'

'Well, if Crane was to marry anyone, I guess it could be her.' He stopped as they heard steps outside and Crane came back. Todd looked around the room and nodded. 'That's better. Now you'd better get moving yourselves, or you won't make it back out of Labyrinth by sunset.'

Crane stood in the doorway, eyes narrowed. 'What're you two conspiring about?' His eyes rested on Tessa's flushed face. 'You look distinctly guilty. Been discussing me behind my back?'

Tessa felt her blush deepen, but Todd's voice was easy as he replied. 'There's a word for people who think that way—it's egotist, ain't it? Believe it or not, Crane, Tessa and me have got other matters to chew over.' He gave the younger man a direct look. 'And we'll find it a whole lot easier once you and your girlfriend are back up on the Rim and all the kerfuffle about bighorn sheep and such has died down. Beginning to wish I never mentioned that track I found.'

He turned back to Tessa, closing one eye in a slow wink, then went on without any change of tone, 'And now, get on your way, the pair of you. I'll be glad of a bit of peace and quiet. Seems a lifetime since I had this place to myself.'

Crane shot Tessa a wry glance and hefted his backpack on to his broad shoulders. Tessa, her lips twitching, followed suit. She followed Crane to the door and hesitated; then, on impulse, turned back.

'Goodbye, Grandfather,' she said, and gave the old man a quick kiss on his leathery cheek. 'We won't be any longer than we can help.'

Todd stared at her. His mouth worked a little; then he set his lips into a firm line and gave her a brief nod.

'Don't have to worry about me,' he muttered. 'I'm accustomed to being alone.' He turned away, going back into the cabin before they had time to move, and Tessa knew that he would not emerge again until he was sure they had gone.

All the same, there was an odd warmth in her heart as she walked away down the track beside Crane. Gruff and irascible Todd might be—but she had a strong feeling that she was getting through to the real man inside. Perhaps, after all, there was a chance of winning him over completely—and even of persuading him to forgive Betsy.

How would Crane take that? she wondered. Would it affect his own hang-ups, would it help him to see that there could be good in love?

Not that it would make any difference to his feelings for her—she knew that. But if it could help him to live a happier life . . .

Tessa shrugged, easing the straps of her backpack. It really wasn't any use worrying about it. Crane was Crane—too independent to change his views just because of her. The best thing she could do was to enjoy the moments she had—this beautiful day, their spectacular surroundings, and no one else around.

It might be the last day they could share in this way. And Tessa determined to make the most of every single second.

'It seems to me,' Crane remarked a little later, 'that you and Grandpa are getting on quite well.'

Together, they were moving along the narrow passage that he had led her along on their first visit to Labyrinth. The warmth of the sun had been cut off by the steep walls, and Tessa felt the chill on her skin.

'I think we're starting to understand each other,' Tessa answered cautiously. 'But he seems—well, almost afraid to give way. I suppose he's held his grudge for so long that he can't let it go so easily.'

'It's not just a grudge.' Crane paused as they squeezed through a gap that was no more than a fissure. 'It's something a bit harder than that to come to terms with. He feels a lot of guilt too, you know.'

'Guilt?' Tess stared at him. 'Why?'

Crane didn't answer at once. It was as if there were

something he needed to come to terms with too—as if, in some strange way, the guilt were his as well as Todd's. 'Well, I guess you ought to know it all,' he said at last. 'It's all tied up with my mum and dad—Joe and Willa. I told you about how they died.'

'Yes.' Tessa's voice was low. What further tragedies had struck at this family, while her mother was far away? Not that she'd been free of tragedy herself—losing her husband so early, fighting a terminal illness now. Tessa looked at Crane, her eyes dark with emotion.

'Well, as I said, it happened not long after your mother went away. A year or so—maybe not that. Grandpa was just getting over it—just about ready to write and tell her he was sorry about the quarrel and wanted to make things up.'

He paused to negotiate a rock and Tessa held her breath. This was something new—that Todd had wanted to make up the quarrel as long ago as that. Before I was even born! she thought. It could have all been over, in the past, before they even had me.

'And then they crashed. They were in a light plane, flying into the Canyon. They hit a cliff and the plane fell into one of the side canyons.' Crane paused again. And when he went on his voice was as dry a a winter leaf. 'It was three weeks before anyone could get in there and find out what had happened. The plane was completely burnt out—they couldn't even find the bodies. The wreckage is still there.' Again, he stopped, looking at Tessa with haunted eyes. 'That's why Grandpa came down here to live—to be near them. It seemed to make him feel—better, somehow.'

Tessa stared at him, horrified. Crane's parents, burned to death down here, the remains of the funeral pyre still lying

in some remote canyon . . . 'But why didn't he write and tell
Mum that?' she asked, her voice breaking. 'Couldn't that
have helped too? Why did it make such a difference?'

'Yeah, that's something I haven't told you, isn't it?'
Crane's mouth twisted a little as he turned again to go on.
'Because he and I—well, we blamed them for the accident,
that's why. Because if it hadn't been for your mum and dad
going off the way they did, they would never have been
down there.' His head snapped round, his hooded eyes dark
upon hers. 'Didn't anyone ever tell you what your dad was
doing around the Grand Canyon?'

For a moment, Tess was at a loss. It was something she
had never asked. 'I thought he was on holiday,' she said at
last.

'Holiday? No—he wasn't on holiday. He was a flier—
didn't you know that? He flew with the airline I run now. It
was a family concern—my dad, Joe, built it up, and your
dad came out to work his way round the world and took a
job with him. That's when Aunt Betsy took up with him,
and then they decided to go back to England.'

'But Dad wasn't a pilot—he was an engineer.'

'And he could fly. Maybe he gave it up, back in England,
but he could fly like an angel, I'll give him that. Matter of
fact, I got on rather well with him—kind of looked up to
him. It was just when he took Betsy away from here and I
saw what that did to Grandpa—and, well, I saw red.'

Tessa shivered, her body chilled. The narrow strip of sky
overhead had darkened and the sheer black walls of the
twisting canyon seemed menacing as they closed in around
her.

'But why did you blame him for Joe and Willa?'

'Because your dad had been trying out some new routes to

fly people—something a bit more exciting than just flying along the Rim. They don't allow it now, or everyone with a plane and a taste for a stunt would be up here, zig-zagging round the rocks. But then, there weren't so many folk about and your dad was always in the Canyon. Anyway, he worked out these new routes, and then he and your mum left and went to England. And it wasn't for a year or so that anyone even dared mention them.' Crane chuckled mirthlessly. 'Grandpa was real mad, I don't mind telling you. And then I guess he started to think a bit straighter, and to realise that Betsy hadn't done anything so very bad, and so things relaxed a bit. And Dad decided to try out some of these routes your dad had figured out, and took Mum along for the ride.'

'And they were killed,' Tessa said softly.

'That's it. At just about the time Grandpa was making up his mind to write.' Crane shrugged. 'After that—right or wrong—well, I guess he just couldn't bring himself to do it. And then it must have seemed too late. He brought me up, and when I took over the airline he moved down here—and tried to forget it all.'

'I see.' The canyon was just wide enough at this point for Tessa to move forward and walk beside him. Tentatively, she touched his hand.

'Would you let me tell Mum all this?' she asked. 'I think if she only knew it all—she could be a lot happier. She would understand—even if Grandfather still couldn't quite forgive her.'

During the silence that followed, she was aware of an odd sound. A far-off rumbling, a pattering, and then a searing flash of light and an ear-splitting crack.

'Thunder!' Crane exclaimed. 'Thunder and lightning—

there's a storm over the Canyon. And here comes the rain!'

Hastily, they scrambled under an overhanging rock, staring at the deluge that had suddenly enveloped them. It was, Tessa thought apprehensively, as if a tap had been turned on—a giant tap, as if the Canyon were an enormous bath that had to be filled as quickly as possible. Water poured down the rocks, polishing them to a sheen of black and red, streaking them with colour from the looser shale above. Already the floor of the canyon was awash, foaming with the force of the storm, and it frothed around their ankles, rust-coloured, cold and muddy.

'Crane!' Tess exclaimed in alarm, and saw that he was staring at the water, his brow seamed with anxiety. 'What are we going to do?'

'Get out as quickly as we can,' he answered curtly. 'This isn't any ordinary storm, Tessa. There must have been a lot of rain higher up for it to soak down as fast as this. There'll be flash floods—and it could be nasty for us if we happen to get in the way of one of them.'

'But Natalee's photographic gear——'

'It'll be all right, that cave stays dry. Come on, girl, no more arguing—we've got to move.'

He set off back the way they had come, ploughing through the water that was already surging along the trail. Tessa followed, glancing anxiously to the side as she went. All the small springs and rivulets that she had noticed yesterday as they tumbled sparkling from the shale, finding openings wherever possible, were now roaring cataracts, gushing water with angry force. How long would it take to fill this narrow fissure? she wondered nervously, and just how far had she and Crane come along it? Immersed in their conversation, she hadn't noticed anything.

And he had been equally involved, or he would surely have noticed the gathering darkness of the sky, the danger signals that would have told him of stormy conditions up on the Rim.

Crane rounded a corner and stopped abruptly.

'Well, that's it, then,' he said, and Tessa peered over his shoulder, suddenly frightened. She drew in her breath.

It must have been less than an hour since they had passed this point. In that time, presumably dislodged from somewhere high above by the pressure of water, a huge rock had fallen into the canyon. As it fell, it had brought more broken rock and debris down with it, and as it had hit the ground it had smashed the walls of the canyon, so that it now formed an impenetrable wall of rock and rubble.

'We'll never get past that,' Crane said, his voice flat.

Tessa glanced wildly over her shoulder. The torrent was fiercer than ever, and the water on the floor of the canyon now several inches deep.

'But what can we do? We've got to get out.'

Crane shook his head.

'No chance that way. And there isn't any other way through to this canyon.' He looked up. 'I don't reckon this is the safest place to stand anyway—there could be more ready to come down. Let's get back a bit, somewhere safer.'

Was anywhere safer? Tessa wondered as she followed him along the rocky passage. Was anywhere safe at all in this deep gash that could be so beautiful and had suddenly turned into a nightmare? Or were they trapped in this corridor, doomed to die here under rock and water, perhaps never to be found again?

Quickly, they made their way back through the maze of gullies that formed Labyrinth Canyon. With water several inches deep now covering the floor, it was more difficult to see the main trail and more than once Crane turned back, saying they had taken a wrong turn. Despairingly, Tessa followed him, fear beating at her throat. Where were they going anyway? Was there even any point in this frantic search for safety, when it seemed that the entire canyon was going to flood?

'We've got to get above the main stream coming from Labyrinth Springs,' Crane told her, gripping her hand. 'That's the one that's most liable to flash flood, and once that goes this whole ravine will fill with water and rock, and it won't be standing still either—we'd be swept aside, there wouldn't be a chance of survival. Once above that, we're pretty safe, and if we can make it to the cave we can even keep dry, there's no water coming down there.'

Tessa hoped he was right, but with the rain now beating at their heads, making it difficult to see, finding the way seemed almost impossible.

She was beginning to think they had lost their way entirely and taken a wrong turning that had led them into an even narrower canyon, a dead-end from which there would be no escape, when Crane stopped suddenly, and Tessa saw that they had arrived at the chasm which had frightened her so much before.

Well, at least they were on the right path. But could she cross that chasm again, in these conditions, even with Crane to help and encourage her?

Tessa peered down and drew back, panic tearing at her mind. The abyss was no longer an empty crack; far below she could see water rushing, thick and black, roaring like a pride of angry lions after some desperate prey. The worn, slender rock of the bridge looked even more fearsome than before, wet and slippery with water streaming across it. One false step, she thought, and you would be over the side, plunging into that foaming void.

'Doesn't look too pretty, does it?' Crane commented. 'Still, it has to be done. I'll go first, then you follow—as quickly as possible, right?'

Tessa trembled. She wanted to refuse to cross the bridge, convinced that it was impossible. Nobody could manage that dreadful six feet, not in these conditions. Even to attempt it would be to invite disaster.

'It's either this or wait to be drowned,' Crane said unemotionally. 'The water from Labyrinth Spring sweeps right across here in flood. You'd be sucked into that——' he nodded towards the abyss '—and you wouldn't have a chance. We've got to get across it and higher up the canyon.'

He moved forwards, put one foot on the narrow bridge. Tessa watched as he stepped carefully across. Then it was her turn, and this time there could be no drawing back; this time, there was no choice.

She took a deep breath and followed his example. One foot—the surface of the bridge was hard under her tread, hard but wet. She could feel the slipperiness.

Another step and she was on the bridge, teetering above the roaring waters, that ran dark and menacing below. Trying to go back now would be even more dangerous than proceeding. Fighting an impulse to close her eyes, she took another step—another—another. She was almost close enough to touch Crane now, and she could see the encouragement in his dark eyes. She felt suddenly better— she *could* do it. Crane stretched out his hand and Tessa, terrified of changing her balance on the wet rock, reached slowly out to take it. She moved—felt her foot slip—grabbed wildly as her balance began to go—and was over, stumbling in panic, falling against Crane, splashing them both with muddy water, clutching at him as she half laughed, half wept in her relief to be on solid ground once more.

'All right,' he said, holding her close with strong, reassuring arms. 'Let's congratulate ourselves when we're safe. We've still got quite a way to go before we get past the spring.'

He turned again and went on up the trail, Tessa following him. The rain was still lashing their faces, the surface water still swirling round their ankles. But although Tessa was aware of the danger, she felt obscurely cheered. They had passed the part that scared her most and nothing else could be quite so bad.

Twenty minutes later they passed the spring, pausing for a moment to stare at it in awe. It was no longer a picturesque cascade, gushing out of a narrow horizontal gap along the top of the non-porous shale. Instead, it had grown—grown into a ferocious gush of water that seemed likely to tear the cliff apart with its force and strength. It no longer ran down the cliff, with spray reaching only a few feet from the stone face, but leapt far out, a gigantic curve of water that arched high above the trail. The pressure was so great that rocks and stones were swept high with the water, flying out from the cliff face, and Tessa could see that it was only a matter of time before a large slab of rock, already ominously cracked, gave way and let more water come surging out.

'Let's get out of here,' Crane said succinctly, and she followed him up the steep, slippery trail that led now directly to the cave.

And it was there, only yards from safety, that disaster finally struck. As they climbed, scrabbling for footholds in the loose surface of the trail, Tessa heard a sudden threatening growl behind her, a growl that swelled and exploded into a violent roar that sounded as if the entire Canyon were falling around her ears. Terrified, she turned to see a mass of water and rock burst out from the face of the cliff, almost animal in its desperate seeking for release. Red with sediment, murky and sinuous, it twisted this way and that, sweeping rocks, trees and shrubs aside with the contempt of tremendous power as it found the easiest way down the valley. It swelled up toward them, reaching almost to their feet, and she shrank back, appalled—had they climbed high enough, were they out if its reach, or was there really no escape? And then, the first tremendous force relieved, it subsided a little. It had carved its way out and was settling into a powerful torrent of foaming muddy water, surging down the gorge and sweeping with it everything that dared to cross its path.

Tessa breathed a sigh of relief and turned to Crane with a shaky smile. But he was no longer standing behind her, powerful, invincible, able to cope with anything fate might throw at them. He was lying at her feet, a long gash on his head, and blood running slowly down his death-white face.

CHAPTER NINE

WITH a cry of horror and disbelief, Tessa knelt down quickly beside the unconscious Crane. What had happened to him? He surely couldn't have fallen, just standing behind her? And how had he got that dreadful cut on his head?

Then she noticed that all round him were rocks—small ones, mostly, brought down by a gush of water that had appeared high up in the wall of the canyon. Another spring had forced its way out from above the layer of shale, bringing debris down with it: only a small one—but enough to be dangerous if you happened to be standing in the way. As Crane had.

Miraculously, none of the stones had hit Tessa, and the roar of the major flood below had drowned the noise. Crane, too, must have been taken completely by surprise as he stood behind her, staring at the chaos just below. He had probably not even known he was in danger.

But there wasn't time to stay here, wondering what had happened. Thick muddy water was swirling round Crane's body and the rain was still lashing down on his face, washing away the blood that seeped from his head. She had to get him up higher, away from the floods, somewhere dry, out of the rain. And the only place was the cave.

Unaware that she was sobbing, Tessa half lifted him in her arms, thankful for his lean figure, but finding it almost impossibly heavy all the same. There was no question of raising him completely; the most she could do was drag him along the slimy track, hoping desperately that she wasn't doing any further damage. But she had little choice. The storm showed no signs of abating and every moment she feared another flash flood that would find them helpless in its path.

The cave was less than twenty yards further up the trail, but the approach was steep and to Tessa it was like climbing Everest. She made it at last and pulled Crane inside, just far enough to lay him carefully on the dry floor. Then exhausted, she collapsed beside him.

But she couldn't afford to rest for long. Crane was still unconscious, and he was cold and wet. He needed to be made dry and warm somehow, and the cut on his head attended to. Fortunately, it didn't seem so bad as it had on first sight; washed clean by the rain, it proved to be more of a surface graze and had already begun to stop bleeding. All the same, it ought to be properly bathed and covered.

What was in their backpacks? Her own, she knew, contained only a small amount of food and fresh water, together with their swimming things, a small towel and a spare sweater. Fingers shaking with cold now, she unbuckled Crane's backpack and found to her relief spare shorts and shirt, a sweater and, best of all, some First Aid kit and a space blanket—a tiny package of material like thin silver foil which would, she knew, open out to form a sheet large enough to wrap him in and keep him insulated by his own warmth.

Thankfully, Tess set to work. She bathed Crane's head with some of the water from her own canteen, and covered it with a pad and bandage. Then, the urgency of the situation sweeping away any possible embarrassment, she undressed him, dried him with her towel, got him into his own dry clothes and unfolded the space blanket. She wrapped his damp clothes in a polythene bag and put it under his head.

By now, she was shivering uncontrollably from shock and cold. Knowing that it would do Crane no good if she were to fall ill, she stripped off her wet clothes, dried herself as best she could with the damp towel, and slipped into her swimsuit, pulling the dry sweater on over the top. That felt better, although her legs were still chilly and she rubbed them briskly to bring the circulation back.

There didn't seem to be anything else she could do. Crane's backpack also contained a small stove and pan, so she could boil water and make a hot drink. But she didn't want to do that yet. There was no knowing how long they might be here, and she couldn't bring herself to drink or eat food Crane might need more desperately when he came round.

If he came round ...

The thought slid like a snake into her mind, and she pushed it away vigorously. He *had* to come round! He couldn't go off and leave her now, just as they'd begun to understand each other. It was just a bang on the head, that was all ... it had to be.

Anxiously, Tessa felt his face and slipped her hand inside the blanket to feel his body. It was warm now, and when she laid her hand over his heart she could feel it beating more strongly. As she gazed down at him, she saw his eyelids flicker ... and open.

'Crane!' she whispered. 'Oh, Crane, thank goodness you're all right. How does your head feel?'

Crane stared at her, his dark eyes bewildered. 'What's been happening? Where in hell are we?'

'We're in the cave—Labyrinth Cave. There was a storm,

don't you remember? We got up the trail just in time to miss the flash flood, but you must have been hit by a rock. How are you feeling? Does it hurt anywhere else?'

Crane moved experimentally. 'Don't think so. Just a God-awful headache. How did I get in here?'

'I dragged you here. I couldn't lift you properly—I just had to hope I wasn't doing you any more damage. We had to get in here, away from the water—it's streaming down the trail.'

'It would.' Crane looked up at her, his eyes still dazed. 'I guess we're stuck here for a while,' he said faintly.

More than a while, Tessa thought, remembering the great slabs of rock that had fallen away from the cliff. A cold fear gripped her heart as she wondered just how they would ever be able to get out, now that the trail was blocked. But she couldn't tell Crane what she was thinking. Instead, she gave him a smile that was shakily cheerful, and grasped at the only straw she could think of.

'Just for a while,' she agreed. 'But it's not so bad. We've got some food here. And Grandfather knows where we are. He'll send help.'

Crane smiled and closed his eyes again, and a moment or two later she realised that he had fallen asleep. Well, it was probably the best thing for him. She only wished that she could do the same.

She went to the mouth of the cave and stared out. The rain had stopped now and blue sky was appearing between the clouds that still hung over the Canyon. But all around her was a scene of complete devastation. Water still ran down the trail and gushed in torrents from the canyon walls. And below, where she and Crane had stood and watched with horror, there was only a clutter of fallen boulders and muddy debris to show where the trail had been. The twisting passages of Labyrinth Canyon had vanished.

Afterwards, Tessa remembered the time she and Crane had spent stranded in Labyrinth Cave as a dark and frightening blur. Only a few moments stood out in her memory: when she'd lit the stove to boil water and make hot drinks, when she'd tried patiently to coax Crane to take some nourishment, when he'd smiled at her and gripped her wrist with a surprisingly strong hand.

And the talk they'd had, deep in the night, with the stars showing brightly again above the canyon and a breathless calm over the storm-ridden valleys.

Waking for the second time, Crane declared himself stronger, his head clearer, the pain no more than a dull ache. He sat up, gave Tessa a somewhat shaky grin, and gulped down the hot drink she made him.

'That's a whole lot better. I must have had quite a crack on the head, to lay me out like that. You did pretty well, Tessa, getting me up here.'

'I was terrified,' she confessed. 'I was afraid if I moved you I might injure you even more badly—but if you'd stayed there, you'd have been swept away, or drowned. And you're so *heavy!* It was like dragging a—a dead horse!'

'Instead of flogging one,' he supplied wryly, and then with a quick glance, 'You must have felt like you were doing that ever since you arrived at Grand Canyon.'

Tessa was taken aback. The dangers and difficulties of the past few hours had wiped all her problems out of her mind. Now they came flooding back—Todd, Betsy, Crane's own attitude that seemed to veer wildly between desire and dislike. But that wasn't strictly true any more, was it? Hadn't they shared many moments of closeness— found an accord that seemed to grow, the more they were together . . .?

Crane was unaware, of course, that Tessa loved him. That was a secret that she couldn't afford to share. And yet . . . As she gazed at him, Tessa wondered whether after all she was right to keep her feelings concealed. Hadn't she already told herself that there must be no more secrets between them—just plain, straightforward honesty? Hadn't everything that happened served to persuade her that nothing else would do?

And now, stranded together in a remote canyon, walled in by a barrier of fallen rocks and surging flood-water— with no guarantee that they would ever be found—was there really room for anything else?

Before she could speak. Crane was raising himself on one elbow, gripping her hand. His agate eyes were smoulder-ing, his face taut, and she could feel the tension in his body.

'Tessa,' he said, his voice throbbing. 'We've got to talk. There are things we need to sort out.' His grip tightened. 'You'll be going back to England soon—when we get out of here. You've done what you came for—Grandpa likes you, he's accepted you, and that's only a short step from opening his heart to your mother too. And you have to go back, don't you?'

Under his gaze, Tessa nodded. 'Yes, I do. I don't know how much time Mum's got now. I can't leave her for too long—and if you're right about Grandfather——'

'I'm right. I know him pretty well.' Crane paused and there was a strange kind of agony in his eyes. 'So that'll be it. You'll go back to England, stay with your mother and probably settle down with some nice English guy. And you won't ever come back to the Canyon again——' He stopped, startled by Tessa's cry of negation, then shook his head, 'No, Tessa, it's true. You won't come back. Oh, maybe for a holiday some time, a few days on the Rim, perhaps even a trip down to see the old man if he's still around. But it won't be the same.'

Tessa said nothing. Inside, her emotions warred together. Everything Crane said was reasonable, logical, could well be true—but there was something he didn't know, something that could make nonsense of it all.

'Crane . . .' she began in a low voice, but already, as if driven by a need too deep to be denied, he was speaking again.

'I just want you to know this,' he said, his voice ragged. 'Wherever you are, whatever happens to you—always remember this one thing.' He took a deep breath. 'I was wrong too, Tessa. Wrong about you, about your mother and father—wrong about love. I know it now. I've been fighting it ever since that first day. I just didn't know what had hit me then, and I didn't like it—and when I realised it could be love, I liked it even less.'

Tessa stared at him. What was he saying? That *he* loved *her*? She shook her head disbelievingly.

'It was like an aching tooth, one you have to keep testing with your tongue. I had to keep trying you, to see if it was real, the effect on you.' He grinned ruefully. 'That's why I didn't want you to come down here too soon—why I insisted on bringing you down by mule, instead of flying you in——'

'Oh, yes!' Tessa remembered the helicopter outside Todd's cabin, the questions that had sprung to her mind and somehow never been asked. 'I wondered about that, when you brought Natalee down. Only I never got the chance to ask.'

'I made sure you didn't,' he confessed with a twinkle that made her want to fling herself into his arms. 'I didn't know how I was going to answer if you did! I still didn't want to admit it, you see—that I really just wanted two days alone with you, watching your face, listening to your voice— getting to know you, building up memories that were going to have to last me through the years . . .'

Tessa listened, mesmerised. Hadn't she been doing exactly the same thing herself? How was it possible for two people to be so close—and yet so far apart?

'It got a bit too much for me to handle once or twice,' he admitted. 'That time in the pool—other times, too, when I nearly lost control. God, you don't know what I was going through then, Tessa. But—well, if any of it caused you any distress, I'm sorry. I never meant it that way.'

'Distress?' Tessa's voice was husky as she slid her hand up his arm. 'Crane, they were the most wonderful moments I've ever known. I didn't know why—I didn't know until just a few days ago that I was in love with you. But when you kissed me, I——'

With a swift, violent movement, Crane sat up. His hands grasped her by the shoulders, his glittering eyes searching hers.

'Say that again?' he demanded hoarsely. '*You*—in love with *me*? Did I really hear you say that, Tessa? Is it really true?'

For a moment, Tessa was sharply aware of the sound outside the cave—the soft rippling of water, the hoot of an owl. Crane's eyes were gimlets in his ashen face. Her own eyes met his with a directness that needed no words.

'Yes, Crane, I love you,' she answered quietly. 'I was going to tell you anyway—even before you started to talk. I felt that there ought to be real truth between us. Even if you didn't want to hear it—even though I knew you didn't believe in it.'

He stared at her and she realised that there had been an indefinable change in his expression, a change that brought life and hope to the lean features and left them strangely softer.

'Didn't believe in it?' he said quietly. 'And just where did you get that idea?'

'You've told me—over and over again. Love's a con, you said—it isn't real—it just causes pain and misery.' She shook her head. 'I've never agreed with you over that.' She raised one hand to stroke tentatively down his cheek. 'I knew that I had to tell you I loved you—because there mustn't be any more misunderstandings. And even if you couldn't love me—well, at least you'd know. People haven't been telling each other enough, Crane. I had to make a start.'

The words tumbled from her lips as if bursting through a dam—as the floods had burst from the rocks during that appalling flood. She needed to tell him all that was in her heart—even if they never spoke of it again.

Crane moved. He drew her into his arms, close against him where she could feel the strong beating of his heart. With one hand, he raised her face to his.

Her heart jerked at the expression in his eyes. Darkened now to the deep brown of a moorland pool, there was an intensity she had never seen in them. His face was grave, un-smiling; yet there was a softness about that firm mouth, a tenderness in the line of his cheek, that belied his gravity. And when he bent his head and laid his lips gently upon hers, she knew that her words had struck some chord deep within him—deeper, perhaps, than anyone had ever reached before.

The world changed as she lay against him, became again the beautiful place it had been before the storm. As they sat close together, silent with wonder, the cave grew lighter. Outside, they could see the brightening of the sky, the first flush of palest apricot, the fire of the sunrise as the Canyon lost its terror and smiled again. What had happened was no more than a brief shiver, it seemed to say, a tremble on the skin of the world; something natural, inevitable, of passing significance only.

This was what was important—the emotion that was being generated between herself and Crane, the love that was growing and blossoming in this strange place, like a new and tender plant.

Crane stroked his lips down Tessa's neck to her throat. His hands were gentle on her body, outlining her curves with a tenderness that had her enthralled, held in an enchantment that it seemed nothing could break. With a sigh, she settled herself against him, delighting in the hardness of his body, pressing her own softness against him. There was very little between them; as he came free of the blanket that she had wrapped around him, Tessa could feel the strength of his bare thighs against her own, the throbbing pressure that told her he was already aroused. The knowledge brought a spurt of excitement to her blood, sending it racing through her pulses, forcing her heart to a crescendo of pounding that had her breathing as rapidly as if she had just run a race, whimpering in her eagerness. With a quick movement, she twisted herself about him, falling back with him on to the pile of clothing that had been their only bedding. Forgetting everything else, she arched her body towards him, wanting to feel him against every inch of her, to know the sensation of his skin against hers, his warmth blending with her own.

'Crane—oh, Crane, I've wanted you so much,' she breathed, and knew that the words were true, even though she had never consciously admitted them until now. All her yearning, all the aching nights, the restless tossing and turning—all were explained as she gave herself up to the passion that seemed to come so naturally when she was with Crane. No wonder they had so often seemed at logger-heads—in each of them there had been this massive source of energy, pent-up until it had to find some release. A release which had come with explosive quarrelling—and with desperate lovemaking, too abruptly terminated.

There need be no termination now. They had both admitted, at last, the feelings that surged within them. Nothing could interrupt them, nothing break in on their consummation. They were, for a time at least, apart from the world, completely isolated in this tiny cave so high up in the inner reaches of the Grand Canyon.

With a tenderness that caught at her heart, Crane laid Tessa on the floor of the cave. He knelt beside her, bending over her as he gently removed her sweater and then the swimsuit beneath it, easing the straps over her shoulders, drawing the soft material down to expose her breasts, rolling it over her stomach and hips, and sliding it with long caressing fingers down her slender legs.

Tessa lay quite still. She watched as he then removed his own shirt and shorts, feeling no embarrassment as he revealed his tanned, muscular body to her gaze. When he knelt beside her again, she stretched sinuously, like a cat, and smiled up at him.

'I love you, Crane,' she said clearly, and saw again that deep, heart-stopping expression of love in his eyes. The look she had seen before but never dared to believe in.

'And I love you,' he said quietly, and then began, slowly, tenderly, to caress her body, letting his fingertips trail lightly over her skin, touching her throat, her breasts, her nipples. Tessa closed her eyes and shivered as he bent to lay his mouth on hers, his lips as gentle as his fingertips, kissing her with tiny, teasing kisses that made her want to cry out for more. But as her agitation grew, he soothed her with murmurings, brushing her hair back with one hand as the other explored further, roving now over her stomach, slipping down to the soft skin of her thighs, pressing gently against her so that Tessa, momentarily calmed, woke to further excitement and moved restlessly in his arms, whimpering with desire.

At that, his control seemed to give way. With a groan that tore its way from his throat, he flung himself full-length beside her, gripping her hard against him. Their legs entwined, they rocked to and fro, each acutely conscious of the body so tightly held. Their lips met again, but there was no gentleness now, only a raging fire of desire and need that had at all costs to be satisfied. Tessa could feel the bruising of his lips, tongue and teeth against hers, and knew that she was digging her nails into his back, but there was no holding back now, no fear of rejection or rebuff. For herself and Crane, this was right—the only way they could express their love, a love that had been frustrated for so long, it had seemed impossible that it could ever be released.

Crane raised himself above her and looked down, a question in his darkened eyes, and Tessa nodded. 'Please,' she whimpered urgently, her senses reeling under that look, under the touch of his fingers, the pressure of his body. 'Please . . .'

And then they were more together than they had ever been before; as close as two human beings can be, their passion thrusting and storming with the same primitive force as that of the tempest that had struck the day before. Tessa was swept away by it into a world she had never dreamed could exist, a world of sensation, delight, and explosive culmination that left her shaking, breathless and in tears. She lay on the hard rocky floor of the cave, cradled in Crane's arms, trembling.

'All right?' she heard him ask in a whisper that sounded oddly unlike his usual voice. 'Tessa, my love, are you all right?'

Tessa smiled up at him, 'As long as you keep calling me that,' she murmured. 'Oh Crane—I never dreamed anything could be so—so——'

'Wonderful?' He looked as shaken as she felt, but his voice held a touch of humour. 'Incredible? Stupendous? Amazing? Have I got there yet? Or—maybe there just isn't a word for it. Maybe no one's ever had to invent one before.'

'All those things and more,' Tessa agreed, and put up both hands to draw him down against her. 'Crane, I don't ever want to leave you.'

'And I don't want you to go.' His eyes were sombre. 'I want you by my side for the rest of my life, Tessa—I've known that for a long time now. But I didn't dream it could ever come true. And it's been driving me crazy.'

He paused, staring abstractedly out over the silent mountains that strode away through the great chasms of the Canyon. 'I said a lot of fool things about love when you first came here,' he said quietly. 'And since then, I've been doing a lot of thinking. I guess I fell for you the moment I saw you walking down that concourse at the airport,' he added with a smile. 'You looked so little, so scared and yet so determined, and you weren't going to let Crane Mellor intimidate you just because he was bigger than you, oh no! You said what you thought and stuck to it; I admired that. And I guess I started to think straight right then.'

'About love?' Tessa asked, and he nodded.

'I was way out about that. But I guess I did have some reason. You see, I fell in love before, once. When I was about eighteen. At least—I thought it was love then. I know different now.' He kissed her nose. 'There's not a lot to tell—she was a spoiled darling, always had everything she wanted, and she happened to want me. And I'd never seen anything like her—up till then, girls hadn't meant anything to me. I'd have done anything for her, Tessa, and she knew it. She played with me—tried to turn me into her lap-dog—and then went off without so much as a glance with some dude from the mid-West. I swore then that I'd never let another girl get under my skin, and I never did—not until now, that is.' He cupped his palms over her smooth bare shoulders. 'I'm not telling you I lived like a monk, all the same,' he added honestly. 'Just that it never meant anything apart from—well, physical pleasure. That's what I was trying to tell you, that first time I kissed you. I'm not proud of that, Tessa—but it backfired on me. I realised then that with you there was something different—and that was when I started fighting.'

Tessa stroked his arm. It was more or less as she had guessed—an unhappy love affair when he was really too young to cope with it. When he'd already had more to cope with than most people face in a lifetime.

'Grandfather told me about your real parents,' she said quietly. 'You've had a lot to face, Crane. It's no wonder you got a bit mixed-up.'

'My real parents?' His eyes went blank, then he looked at her with something like anger. 'Don't ever call them that, Tessa. Those people—they just happened to give birth to me, that's all. Joe and Willa were my real parents. They were the ones who gave me a home, love and a family—Grandpa, your mother, you. I never even *think* about those other people—and I never talk about them. There's nothing to say.'

Tessa was silent. It would have been surprising, she reflected, if Crane could have disposed of all his traumas with one fell swoop. What had happened to him in childhood had bitten very deep, and maybe he would never be able to talk about it fully, even to her. But that didn't really matter now. It was the future that was important—not the past.

'I fought against you, Tessa,' Crane went on. 'I still couldn't tell the difference between real love and what happened with that other girl. I thought it would be like that all over again, and I wasn't prepared to let it. I wasn't going to be *anybody's* lap-dog!'

'You won't be,' Tessa said, smiling. 'I don't like lap-dogs. I like big, husky brutes that knock you over because they love you so much, and guard you with their lives.'

'And that's just what I'll do,' Crane promised, taking her in his arms again. 'I'm seeing straight now, Tessa, my darling. And if I hadn't already—well, there was a time or two back there in that flood when I thought I was going to lose you, without ever having told you the truth. That brought me to my senses. I never want to go through anything like that again.'

'Nor do I.' Tessa thought of the moment when she had looked down to find Crane at her feet, bleeding and unconscious, and shuddered. She drew closer to him and they sat close together, their love beating strongly between then. The urgency had gone now; they were content in the knowledge that they had the rest of their lives before them. Lives that would be filled with adventure, with delight, with laughter and love.

There was just one more thing Tessa had to know.

'Crane,' she said tentatively, 'what about Natalee? Doesn't she—won't she be expecting . . .?' She didn't know how to finish the sentence, and let it trail away. And when she saw Crane's eyes on her, bright with amusement, she flushed and laughed a little. 'Well, you know what I mean!'

'You mean she'll be expecting me to say things like this to her?' Crane's mouth twitched and widened into a grin. 'You think she might be disappointed? Well, quit worrying, Tessa, honey. Natalee's going to be over the moon when she hears we're getting married—we *are* getting married, aren't we? I don't think I've actually asked you that yet. Anyway, she's been nagging me to do that for—well, I don't like to tell you how long.'

'Natalee has? But—didn't you—weren't you——?'

'No, we weren't, not ever. Best of friends, yes, but anything more?' Crane shook his head decisively. 'I guess we've been brought up too close for that—almost like brother and sister. Nat's parents did a lot for me after mine died, you see. And although she's younger than me—well, she kind of took me over then and she's never let up. She's been telling me the kind of things you told me for years, but I never took any notice. And then when I told her about you—well, I reckon she saw there was something different about you and decided you must be the one. That's why she made me bring her down to Grandpa's. She said there was no sense at all in me being topside while you were down there, and if I needed an excuse to be around—well, there was the photography. And when she saw that you were just as bad as I was, pretending there was nothing between us— well, I guess she decided to ginger things up a little, and make out she was after me. She's got a strong romantic streak in her, Natalee has, though you'd never think so to look at her. Reads a lot of women's magazines, love stories and all that stuff.'

'And what's wrong with that?' Tessa demanded severely. 'It might do you a little good to read some, some time—not that you seem to need too much teaching,' she added faintly, as Crane stopped her words with a kiss, his lips moving sensually against hers, tongue flicking into her open mouth. 'Crane—oh, Crane, my love . . .'

But even as they slid down together to lie once again entwined on the floor, the thundering vibration of an engine outside told them that this time they would not be left in peace. Tessa gasped, covering her ears with her hands, and Crane jerked himself upright. Bemused, they stared at each other.

'What——?' Tessa began, but Crane broke in, his expression a mixture of delight, relief, and plain frustration. 'It's the helicopter!' he told her, reaching for his clothes. 'It must be Emery—Grandpa's got a message up to tell him where we were heading and he's searching for us. Come on, Tessa—get out there and wave, or they'll miss us!'

Dragging on his shorts, he bounded out of the cave's entrance. Dazed, Tessa pulled on her swimsuit and sweater, following him. For the past few hours, as she and Crane talked and made love, she had forgotten that they were stranded, forgotten everything but the joy of being at last in accord with the man she loved. But now she remembered— remembered that they could, if not found soon, stay here for days. Or even longer. Long enough to starve.

Shivering, she went out to the rocky plateau in front of the cave and stared around her. The flood had subsided, leaving the trail muddy but dry. But there was still no way out. Below, she could see the tumbled mass of boulders that blocked the entrance to the canyon. Many of them were immense, great slabs of cliff that had been torn away from the canyon walls by the pressure of the water behind them. There was no possible chance of clambering down them, and even if there had been, no knowing what dangers might lie out of sight.

But above, hovering close to the precipice, was the welcome sight of Crane's helicopter, so close now that Tessa could see Emery's face peering down, split with a wide beam of relief at seeing them both safe. He waved and shouted something which was obliterated by the thunderous noise of the helicopter's engines.

'Get ready for a ride,' Crane said cheerfully, as Emery wound down the rope that would winch them up into the safety of the hovering craft. He held her between his hands for a moment and looked down at her. 'It's back to civilisation now, Tessa,' he said in a quiet tone. 'But we'll always remember this night, won't we?'

'Always,' she assured him, and reached up to draw his head down to hers. And, even above the noise of the engine, quite distinctly heard Emery cheer.

'So you're gettin' wed?' Todd Mellor stuffed tobacco into his already overflowing pipe and glinted a look at Tessa from under his shaggy brows. 'Well, I guess we saw it coming, Natalee and me. And I guess you could do a whole lot worse, the two of you.'

Tessa and Crane smiled at each other. They were sitting close together on the big sofa in Crane's bungalow, the smell of roast turkey and apple pie still lingering in the air, mingling with the aroma of the coffee and liqueurs that stood before them on the low table.

It seemed a long time now since they had been stranded together in that dark cave, surrounded by the tumbled rocks of the Canyon. Tessa thought back to all that had happened since—the rescue by helicopter with the flight out of the Canyon, back to the rim, the meeting with Todd there. He had been brought up first of all, found by Emery when he had flown in with the urgent news that Tessa's mother had been taken to hospital. By then, with the storm's damage apparent, it had become vital to find Crane and Tessa, and Emery had searched the canyon, recognising little of the landscape after the floods and landslides.

'We thought you were dead,' Todd had said over and over again, clutching them both to him with trembling arms. His voice had shaken too, as for the first time in years he allowed his emotions to take charge. 'Thought I'd lost you, like I lost all the others.' His old eyes had scanned Tessa's face as if even now he could not quite believe that she was back with him. 'Girl, this last night's been a lifetime to me. I didn't know I could hurt so much. If she's gone, I kept saying to myself, if she's gone without me ever having told her . . .' He blinked rapidly. 'Well, I'm going to tell you now. I was wrong—I was wrong all along. I blamed your mother for everything bad that ever happened to me after she went. Didn't matter what it was; I'd have blamed her if the darned cat had got run over. I guess I just went right off my head—and I was never right again until I went down in the Canyon to live.'

He paused. There were people all around them, visitors queuing for flights through the Canyon, airport workers passing to and fro. Todd didn't seem to notice any of them. He went on, speaking quickly, his voice gruff with tears he'd bottled up for over twenty years.

'I guess I knew for a long time that Betsy didn't really do anything bad when she went away. Maybe she was right—I was too strict with her. It was her life—she had a right to spend it the way she chose.' Tessa felt Crane move closer to her, and felt for his hand. 'I read all her letters, you know—kept 'em, too. In a queer kind of way, I lived for those letters—but I couldn't quite bring myself to write back. I don't know why; just a stubborn old man, I guess. And then you came—and it was Betsy all over again.' The sinewy hands gripped her arms. 'If I'd lost you, down there in the Canyon, I just dunno what I'd have done,' he said in a whisper.

Tessa stirred and reached out for her coffee. That moment of emotion had passed, leaving herself and her grandfather with a depth of understanding that was no less comfortable for being unspoken. Todd would never change now, she knew. He was never likely to express himself in quite that way again—but it wouldn't matter. He'd said what she wanted to hear, and he would never take it back.

'It was a lovely welcome-home meal,' she said, smiling at Natalee. 'Thank you very much. And—thanks for everything else, too.'

The two girls exchanged a look of perfect understanding and Tessa felt the warmth of knowing that she had made a friend. She looked round the big, softly lit room. She had found more than a friend since the first time she had walked in here, rigid with tension and doubt. She had found a sense of family in her grandfather, and a lover in Crane.

'So when's it going to be?' Todd pursued. 'S'pose you're in a tearing hurry, like all the rest? Any chance of me getting to give the bride away?'

Tessa gave him a smile of delight, but it was Crane who answered. 'We're not sure yet when it'll be,' he said. 'Or where. I haven't found out yet what the situation is— whether Tessa can marry here, or whether it would be easier to go back to England. But you're right—it'll be as soon as possible. I never heard that you hung about much, when you married Grandma.'

Todd glowered at him. 'We waited the full year, like her contract said,' he objected, and shrugged as they all laughed. 'Well, I don't say but what I wouldn't have liked it to be quicker . . . Anyway, that's neither here nor there. I guess you'll be going back to England too, to see Betsy.'

'Yes, and that must be soon, too.' Tessa's face clouded. The anxiety she had felt when hearing the news that Emery had brought, that her mother was in hospital, had been followed by relief when she rang England to discover that the emergency was over, and Betsy stronger then she had been for some time. But there was no real comfort to be had—Betsy's time was still short and Tessa was feeling increasingly that she ought to be back with her mother. 'We're booking the first flights available—so if we can have the wedding before then, it'll be our honeymoon.' She smiled at Crane. 'I know Mum's going to be delighted.'

Todd cleared his throat. 'And is there any chance of me getting a flight too?' he demanded gruffly, adding when he saw their astonished faces, 'Well, there's no need to look like that! Can't I go and visit my own daughter if I've a mind too? I'm fit and well, ain't I? Not too old? Or maybe you don't want an old man along on your honeymoon. Sounds pretty funny, I'll allow.'

Tessa got up and ran across to her grandfather. She dropped on to the arm of his chair and bent to kiss his cheek. There were tears in her eyes, and one of them fell on to the back of his brown, leathery hand.

'Of course we'd like to have you along,' she said softly. 'It's a wonderful idea—and Mum will be thrilled. It's the best thing you could do for her, and the best wedding present you could give us. Isn't that right, Crane?'

'That's right,' Crane said, his voice firm, and Tessa raised her head to look at him. For a few moments they were all silent, savouring the wonder of all that had happened—the forgiveness of Todd for his daughter's elopement, the deep love that had grown and was still growing between Tessa and Crane. The new life that was about to begin for all of them.

There would be sadness to come, as well as joy, Tessa knew that. But the sadness was somehow a part of the rhythm of life, a rhythm expressed by the Canyon itself and the changes that were wrought in it—some gradual and gentle, some sudden and devastating—over the years.

Nobody had the right to expect perfect happiness. All you could do was make the best of what came your way, living your life with love and tolerance, accepting the right of others to do the same. And with no secrets, she thought, going back to the sofa and settling down once more beside the man she had promised to marry.

No secrets. But would she ever—*ever*—be able to tell him just how much she loved him?

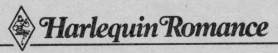

Harlequin Romance

Coming Next Month

Available in January wherever paperback books are sold, or
through Harlequin Reader Service.

In the U.S.
901 Fuhrmann Blvd.
P.O. Box 1397
Buffalo, N.Y. 14240-1397

In Canada
P.O. Box 603
Fort Erie, Ontario
L2A 5X3

Can you keep a secret?

You can keep this one plus 4 free novels

Coming Soon
from Harlequin...

GIFTS FROM THE HEART

**Watch for it
in February**

HEART-1
February 88